Ria!



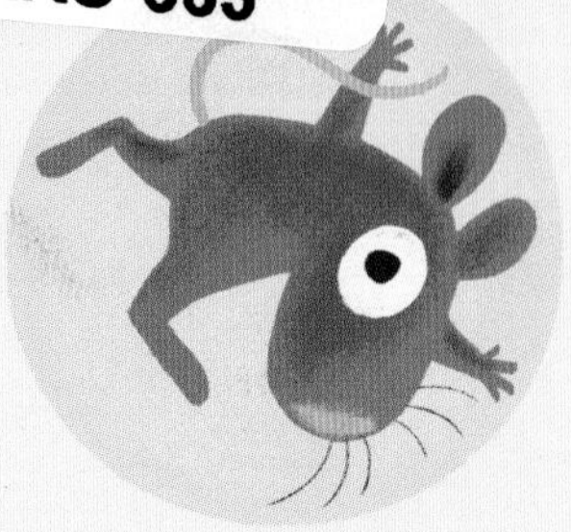

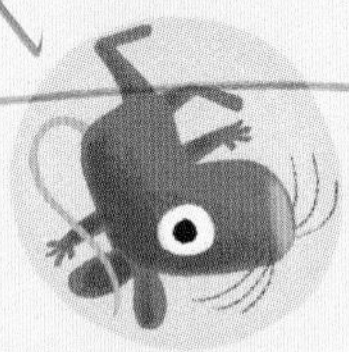

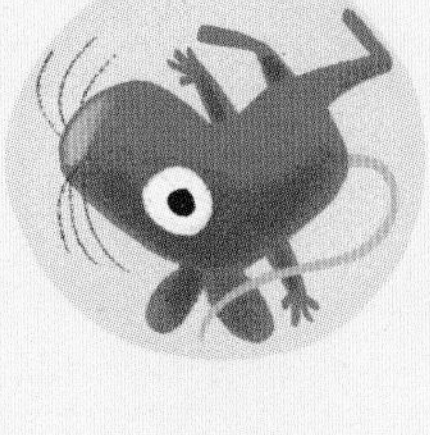

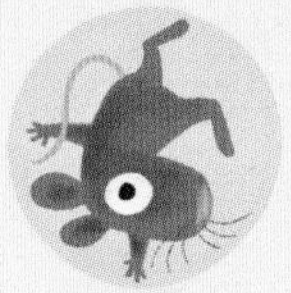

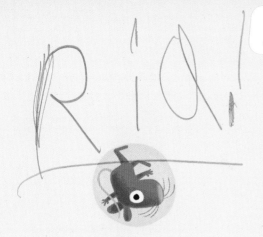

Also look for:

BOBO AND PUP-PUP: LET'S MAKE CAKE!

# BOBO and PUP-PUP

## WE LOVE BUBBLES!

by Vikram Madan

illustrated by Nicola Slater

A STEPPING STONE BOOK™

Random House 🏠 New York

For Madhu, who believes in me, more than anyone
—V.M.

To Leo and Finn
—N.S.

Text copyright © 2021 by Vikram Madan
Cover art and interior illustrations copyright © 2021 by Nicola Slater

Visit us on the Web!
rhcbooks.com

Educators and librarians, for a variety of teaching tools, visit us at RHTeachersLibrarians.com

*Library of Congress Cataloging-in-Publication Data*
Names: Madan, Vikram, author. | Slater, Nicola, illustrator.
Title: We love bubbles! / by Vikram Madan ; illustrated by Nicola Slater.
Description: First edition. | New York : Random House Children's Books, [2021] |
Series: A stepping stone book | Audience: Ages 4–7. | Audience: Grades K–1. |
Summary: Pup-Pup loves blowing bubbles and does not like having best friend Bobo pop
all of them, but when Pup-Pup uses super-strong bubble mix, bubble trouble ensues.
Identifiers: LCCN 2019050352 (print) | LCCN 2019050353 (ebook) | ISBN 978-0-593-12065-1
(hardcover) | ISBN 978-0-593-12066-8 (library binding) | ISBN 978-0-593-12067-5 (ebook)
Subjects: CYAC: Bubbles—Fiction. | Friendship—Fiction. | Monkeys—Fiction. | Dogs—Fiction.
Classification: LCC PZ7.1.M2589 We 2021 (print) | LCC PZ7.1.M2589 (ebook) | DDC [E]—dc23

MANUFACTURED IN CHINA
10 9 8 7 6 5 4 3 2 1
First Edition

# Contents

# Chapter 1
# Bubbles!

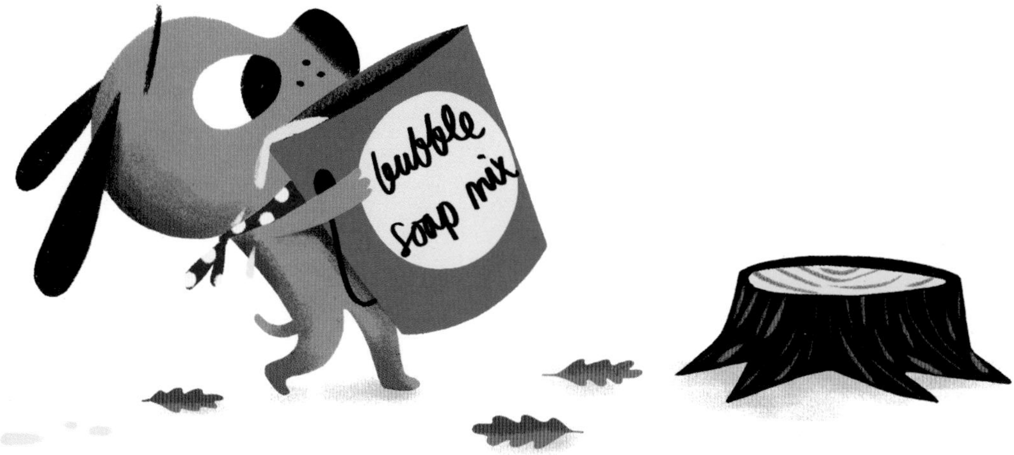
bubble
soap mix

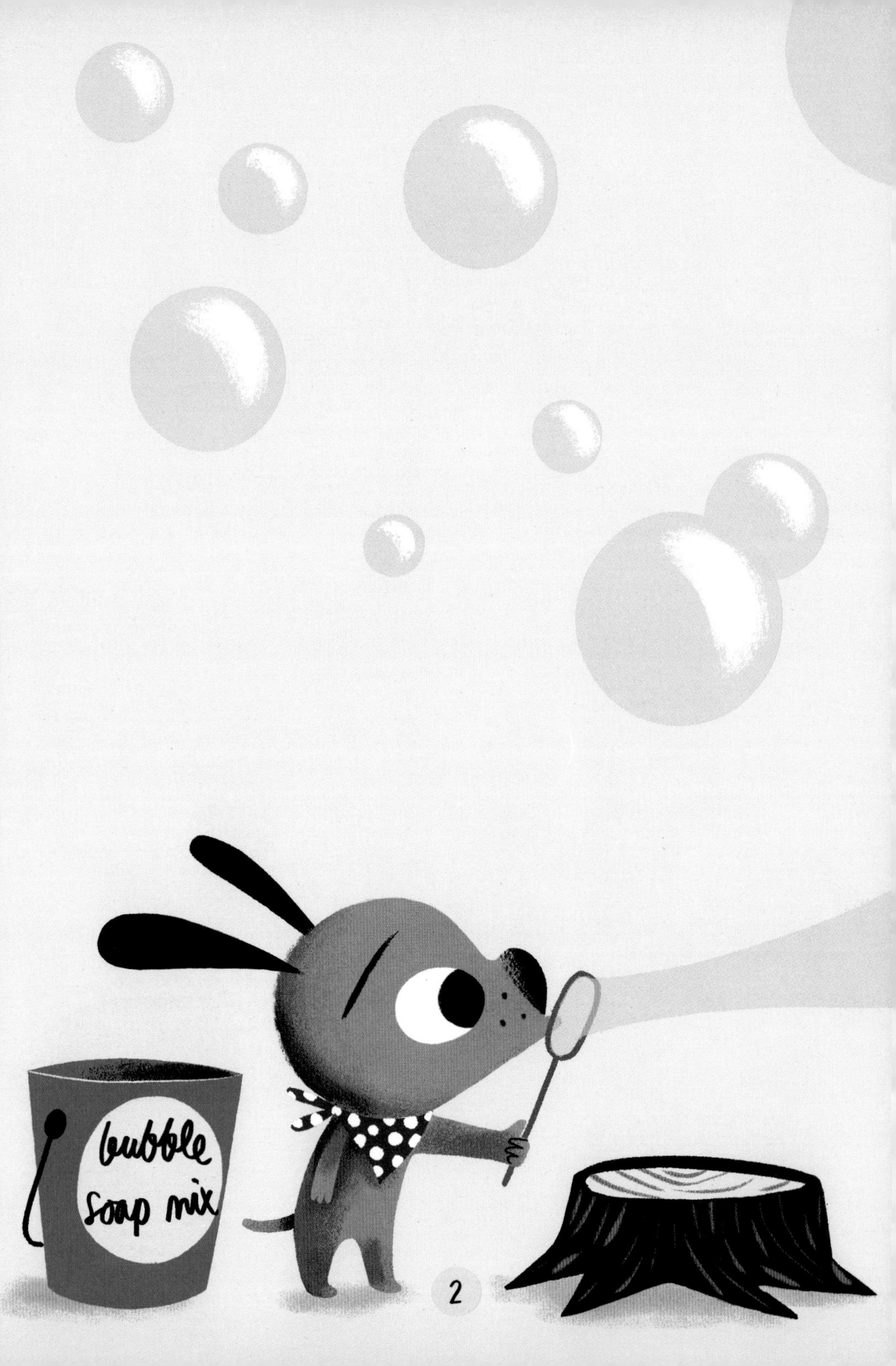
bubble
soap mix

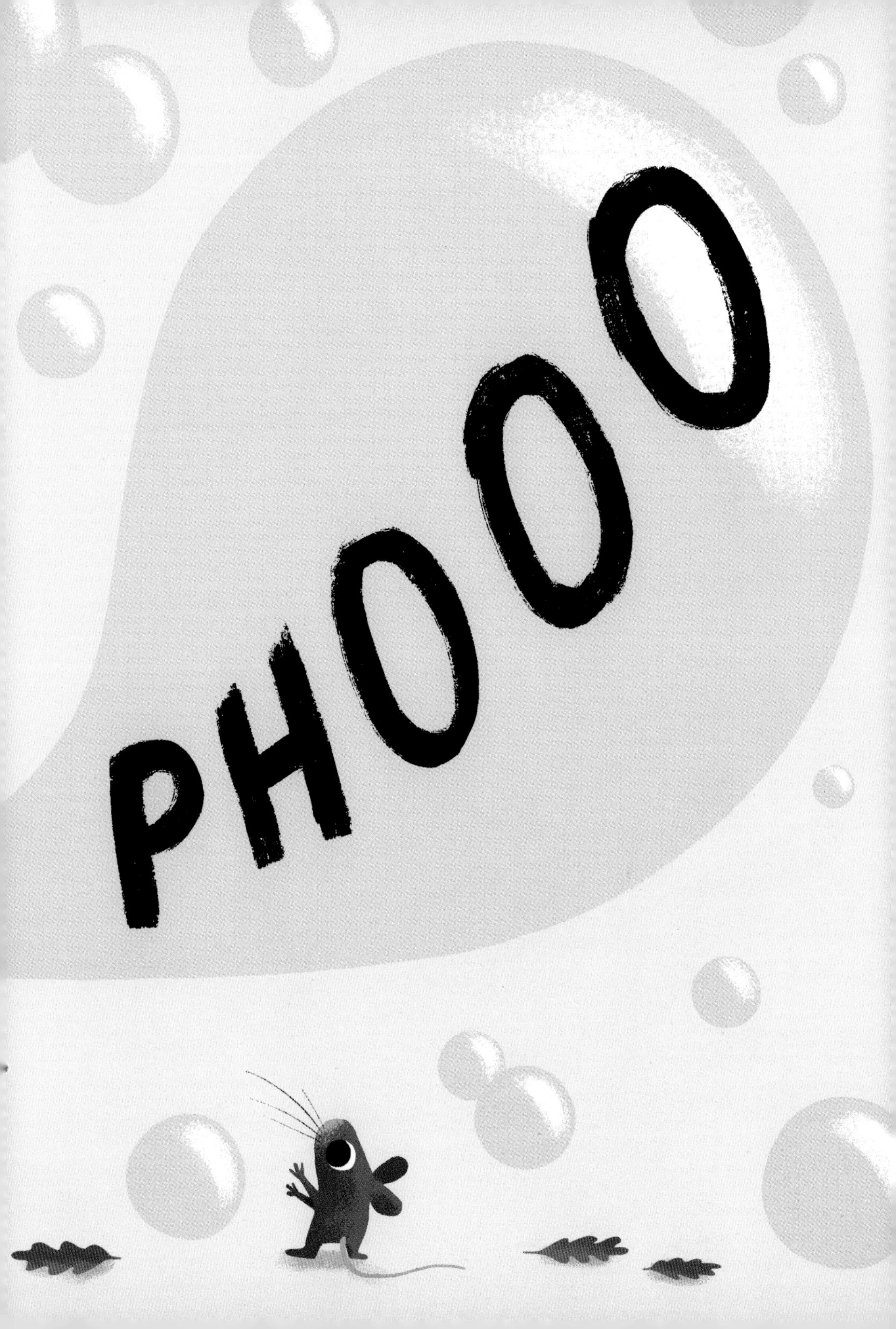
PHOOO

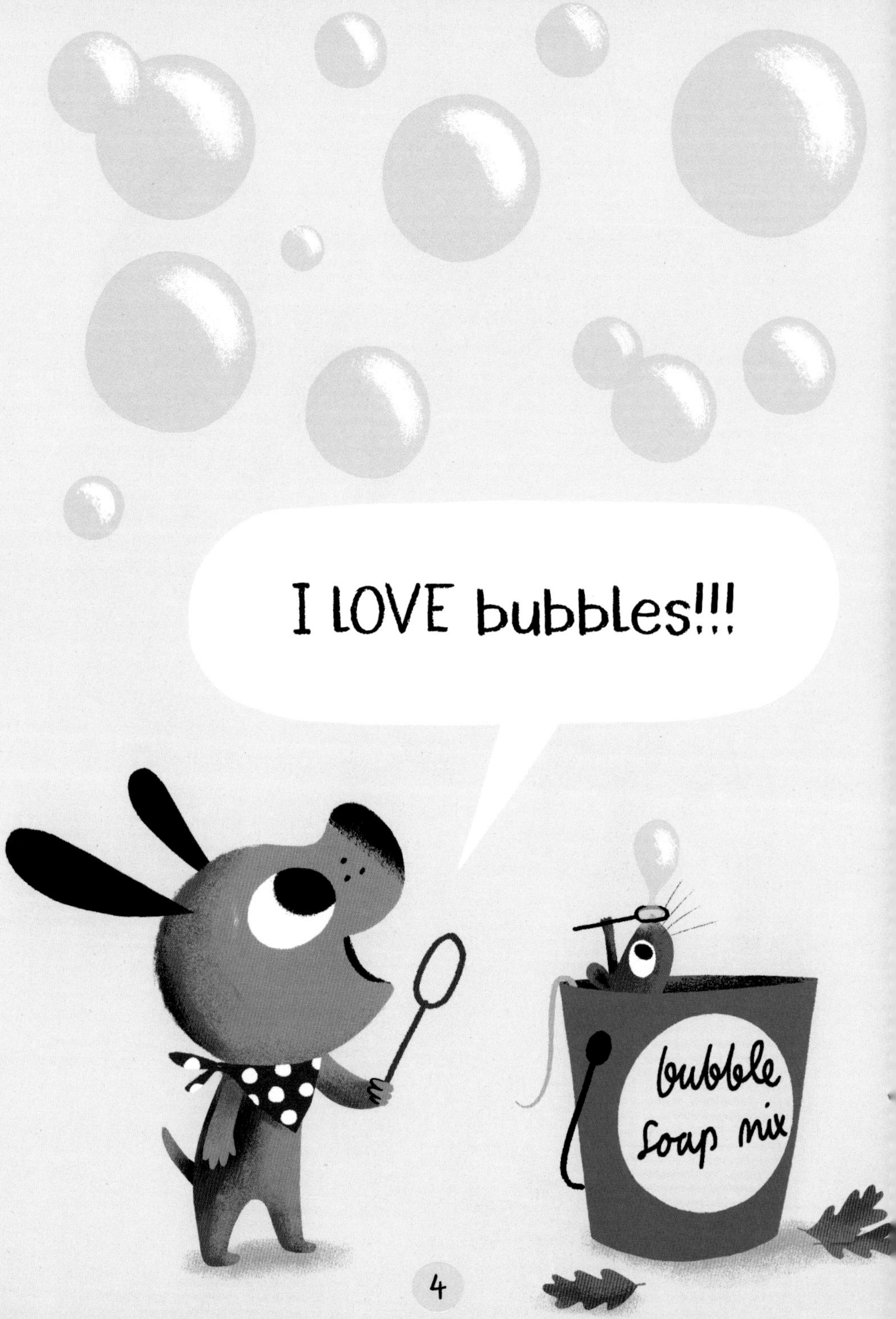
I LOVE bubbles!!!
bubble soap mix

BUBBLES?
I LOVE bubbles, too!!!

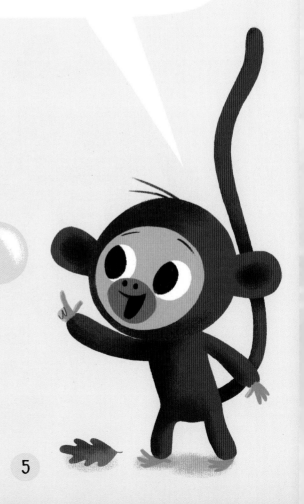

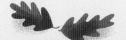

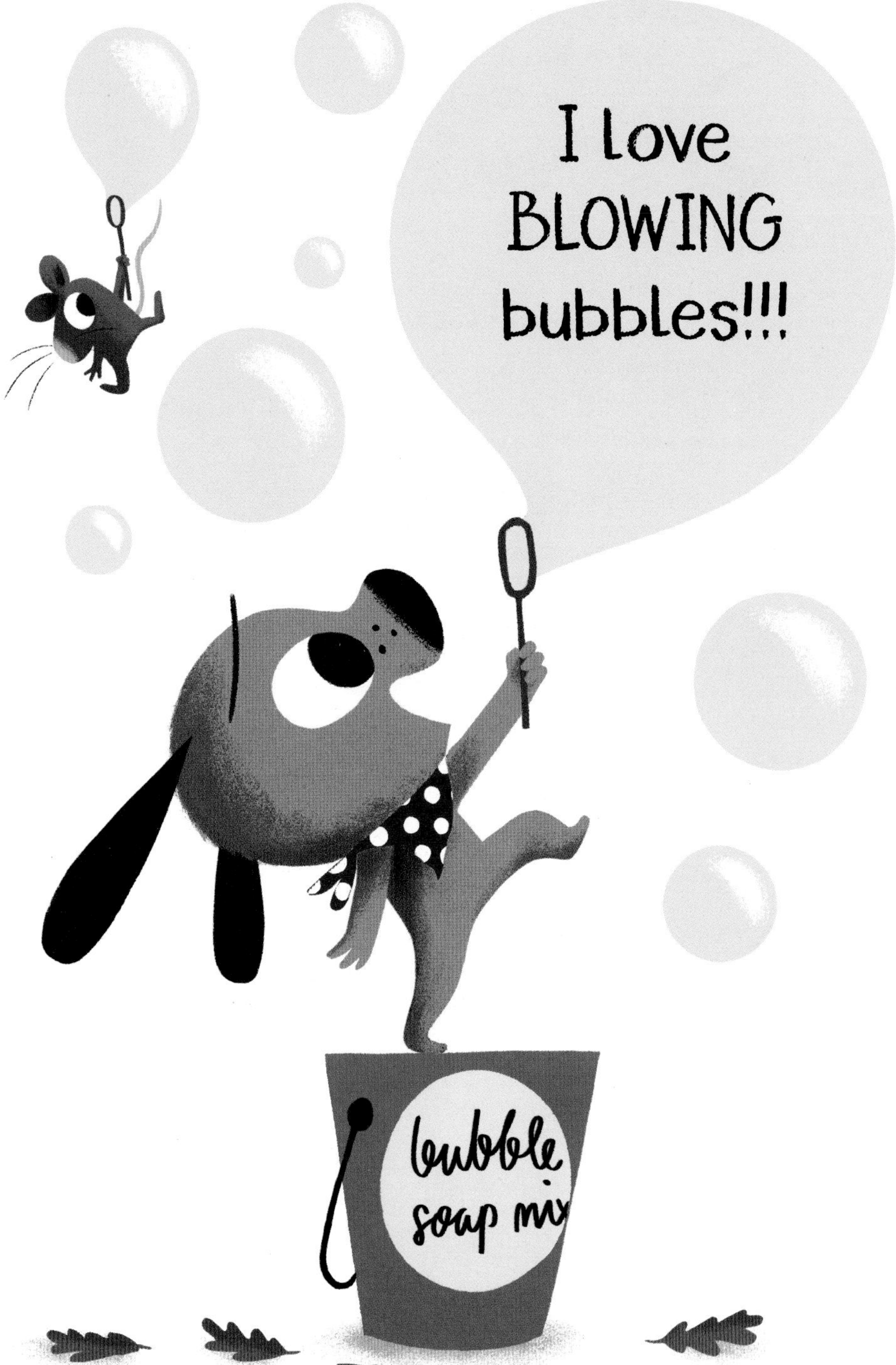
I love
BLOWING
bubbles!!!
bubble
soap mix

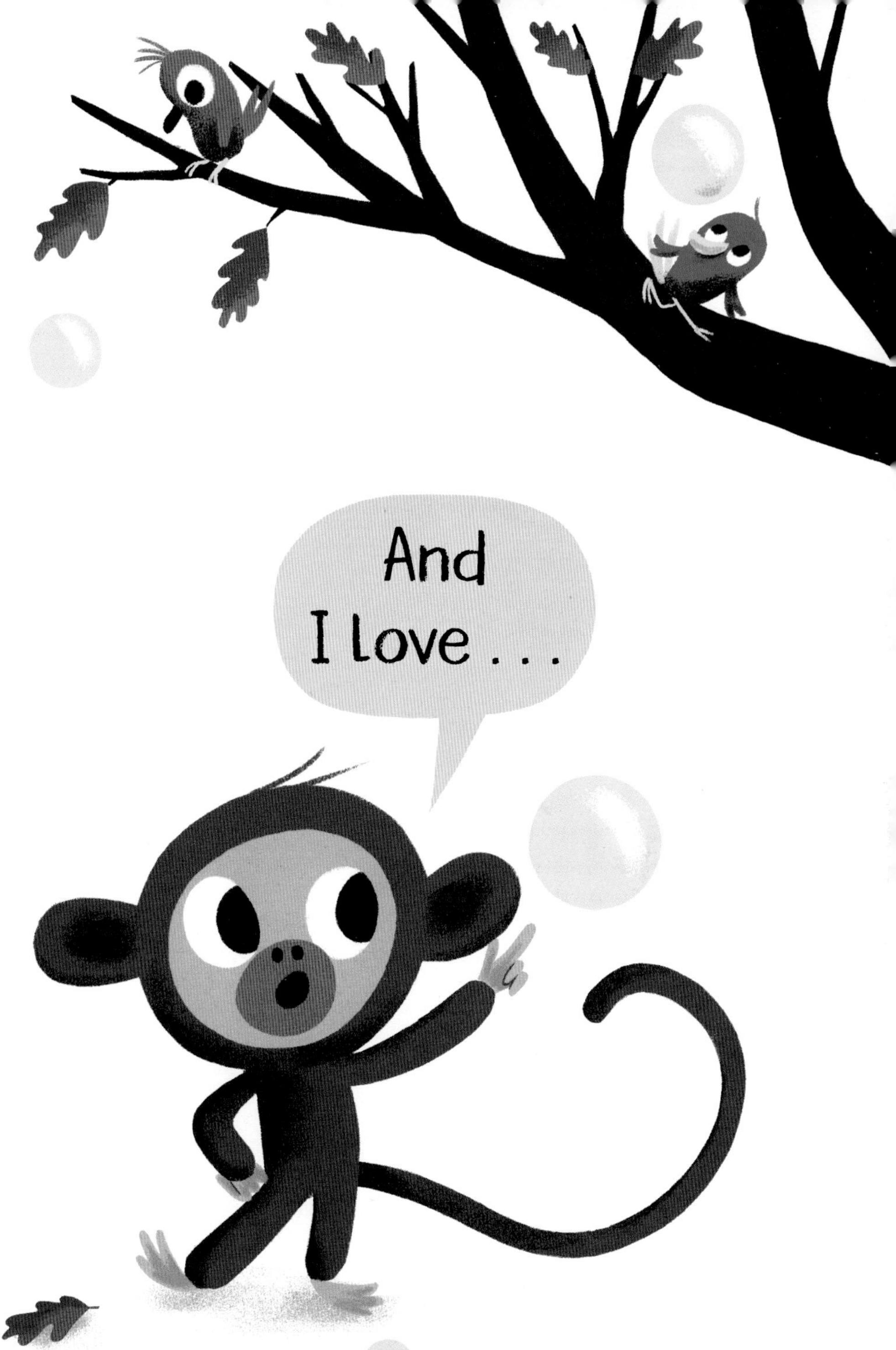
And
I love . . .

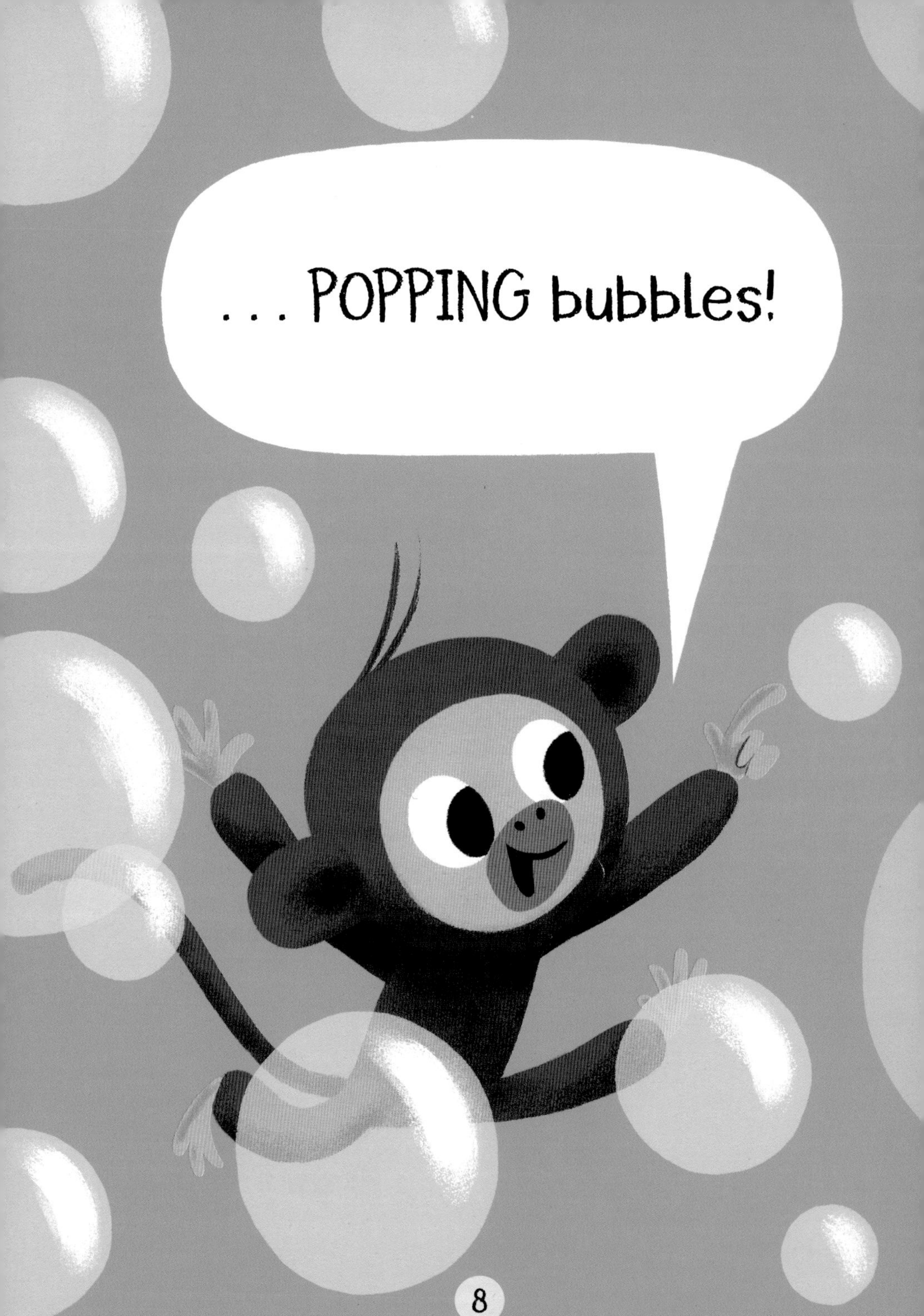
. . . POPPING bubbles!

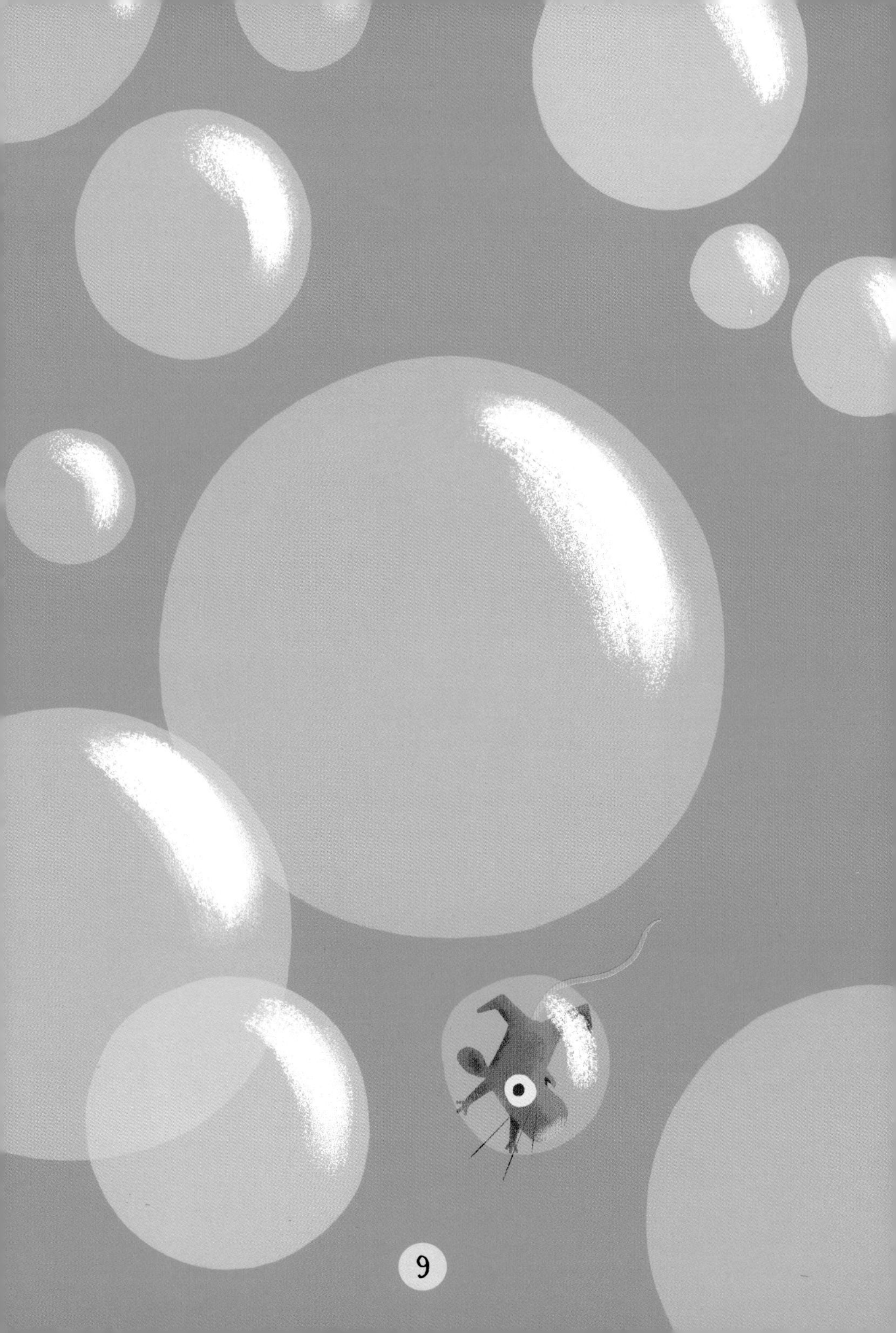

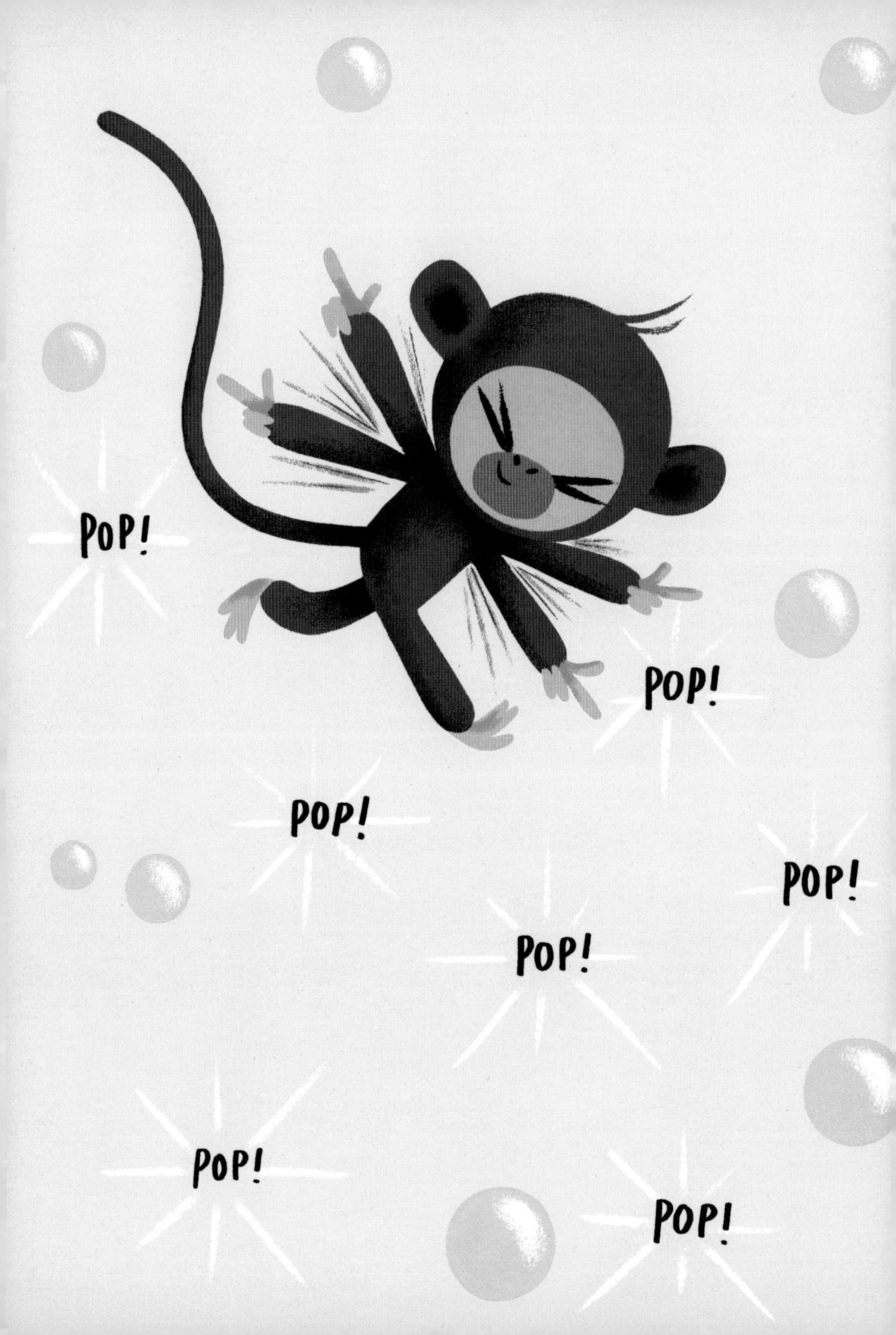
POP!
POP!
POP!
POP!
POP!
POP!
POP!

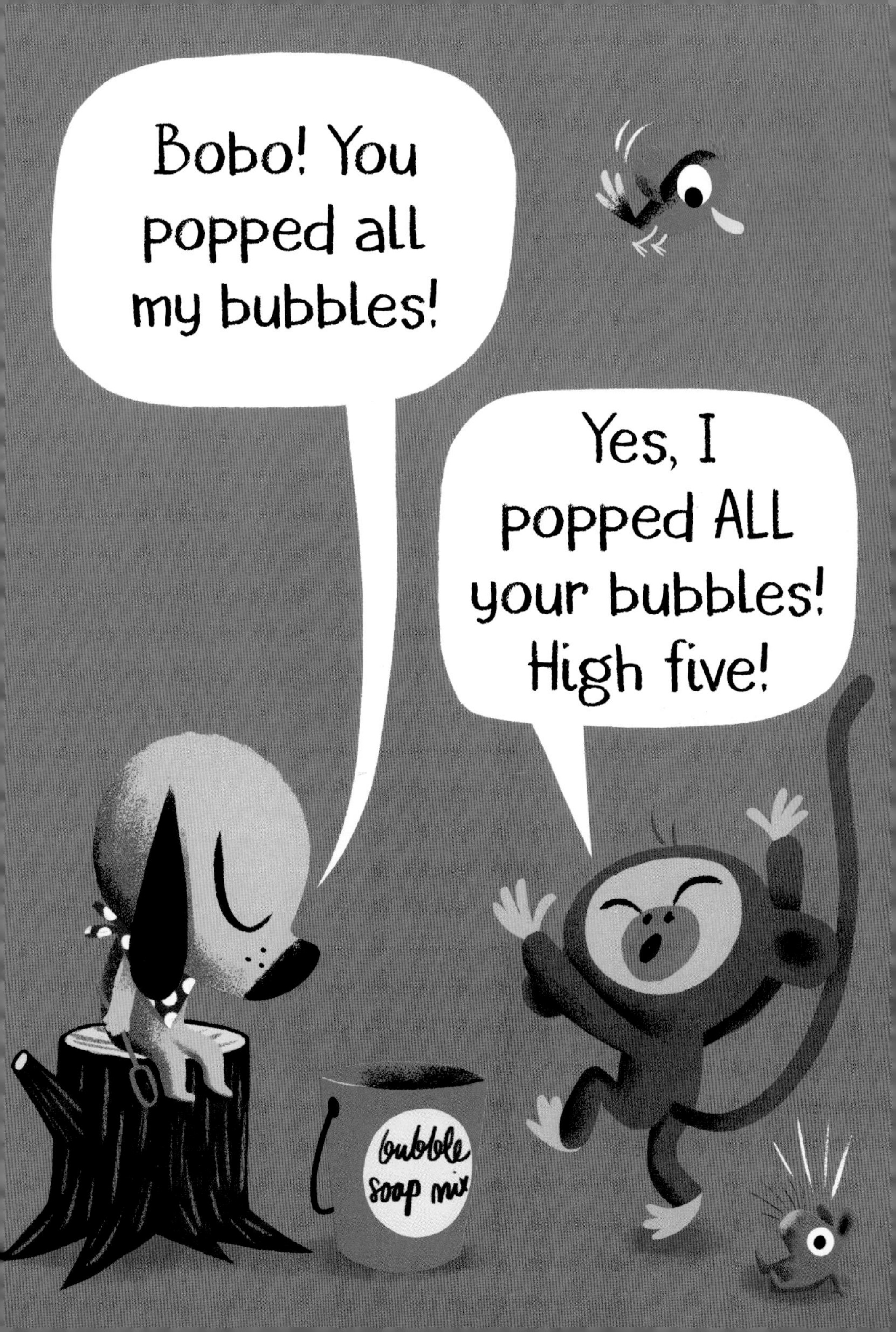
Bobo! You popped all my bubbles!
Yes, I popped ALL your bubbles! High five!
bubble soap mix

# Chapter 2
# MORE Bubbles!

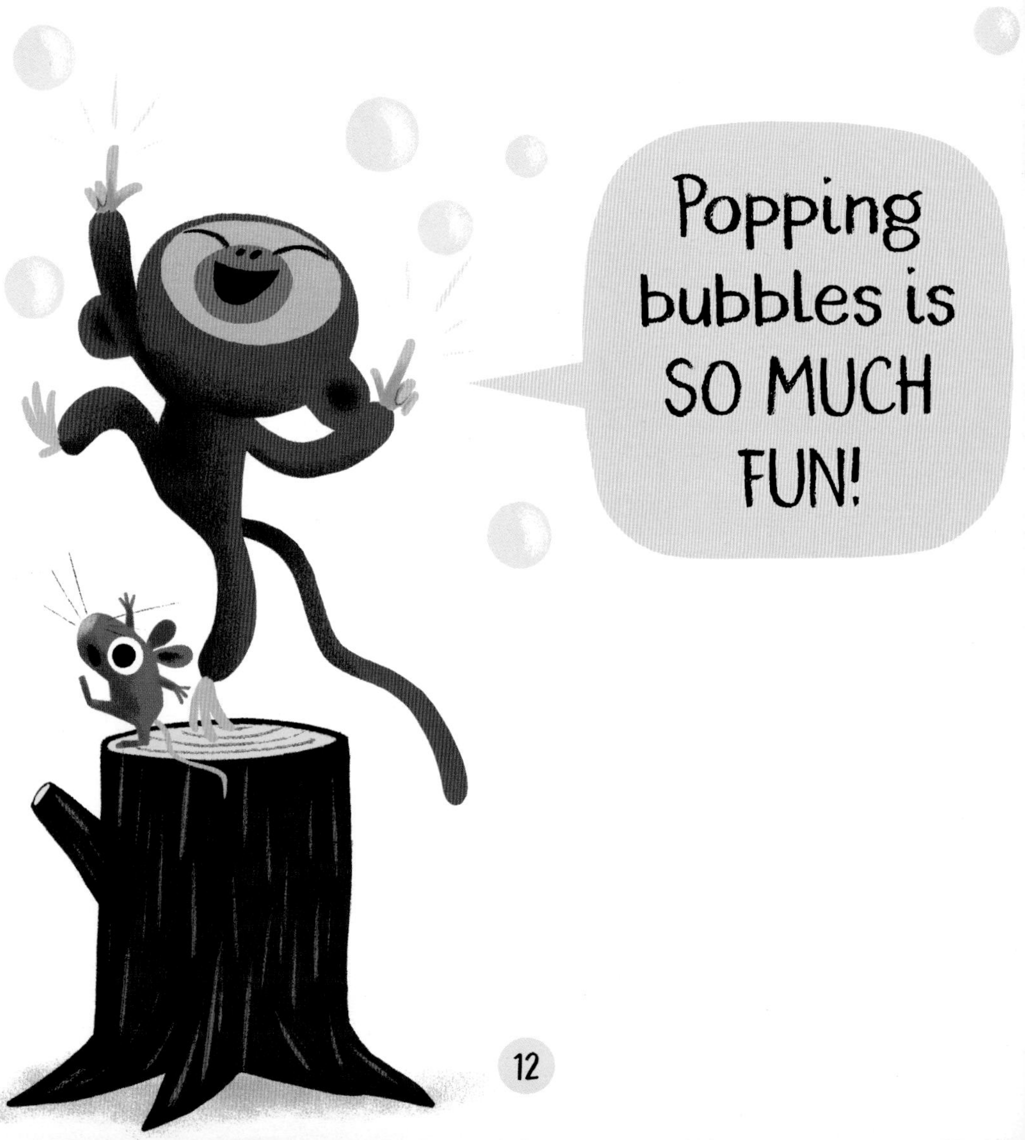
Popping bubbles is SO MUCH FUN!

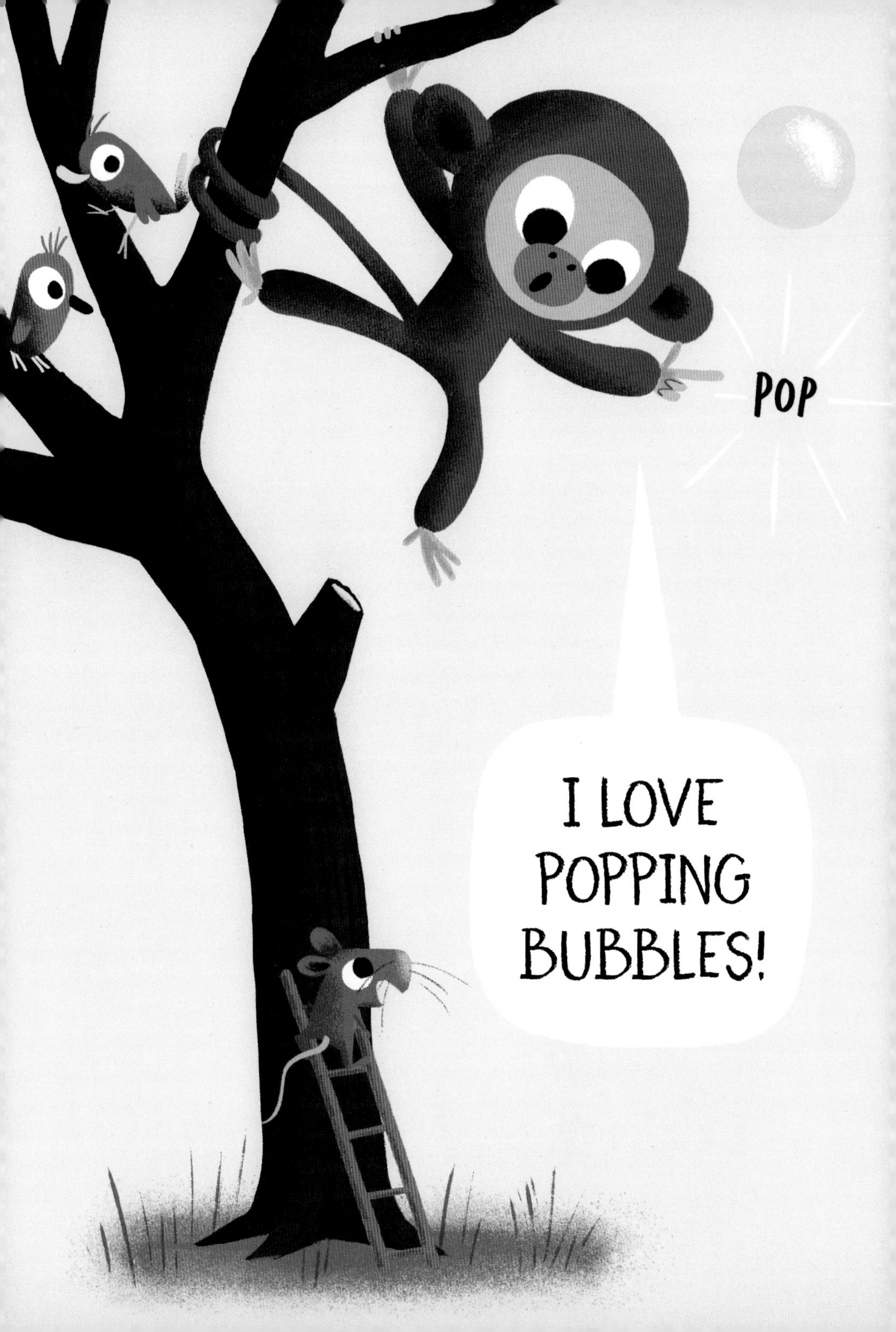
POP
I LOVE POPPING BUBBLES!

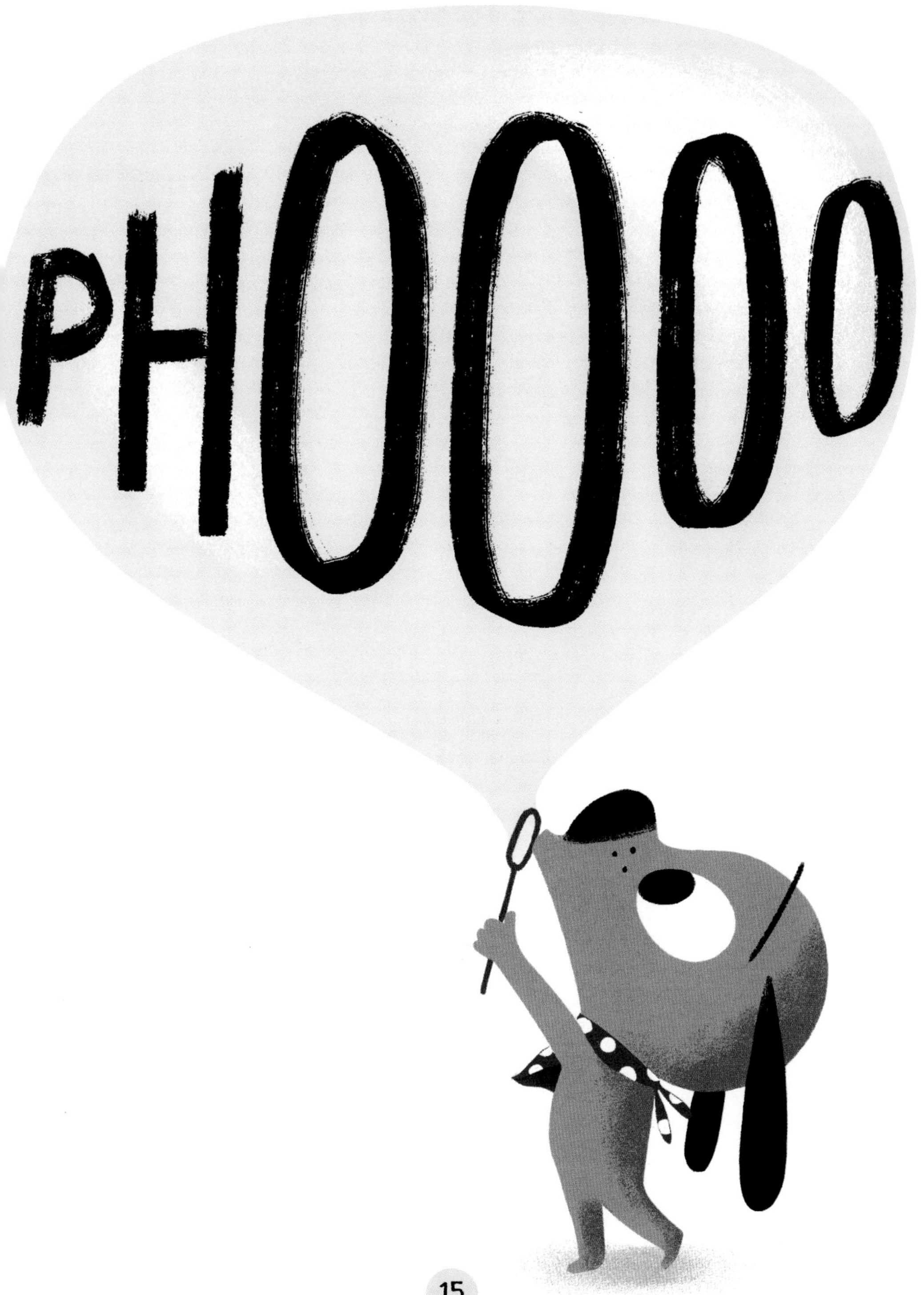
PHOOOO

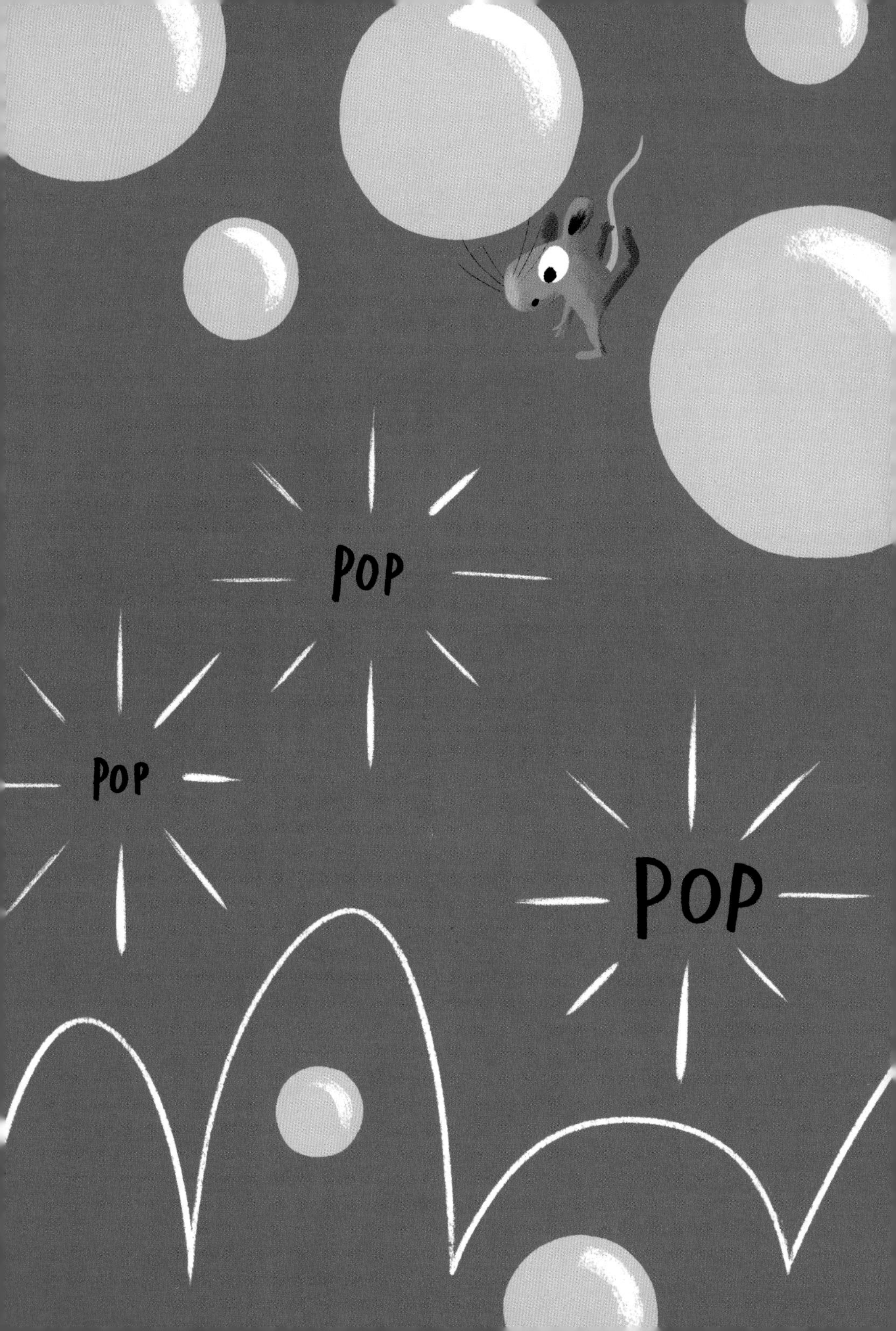
POP
POP
POP

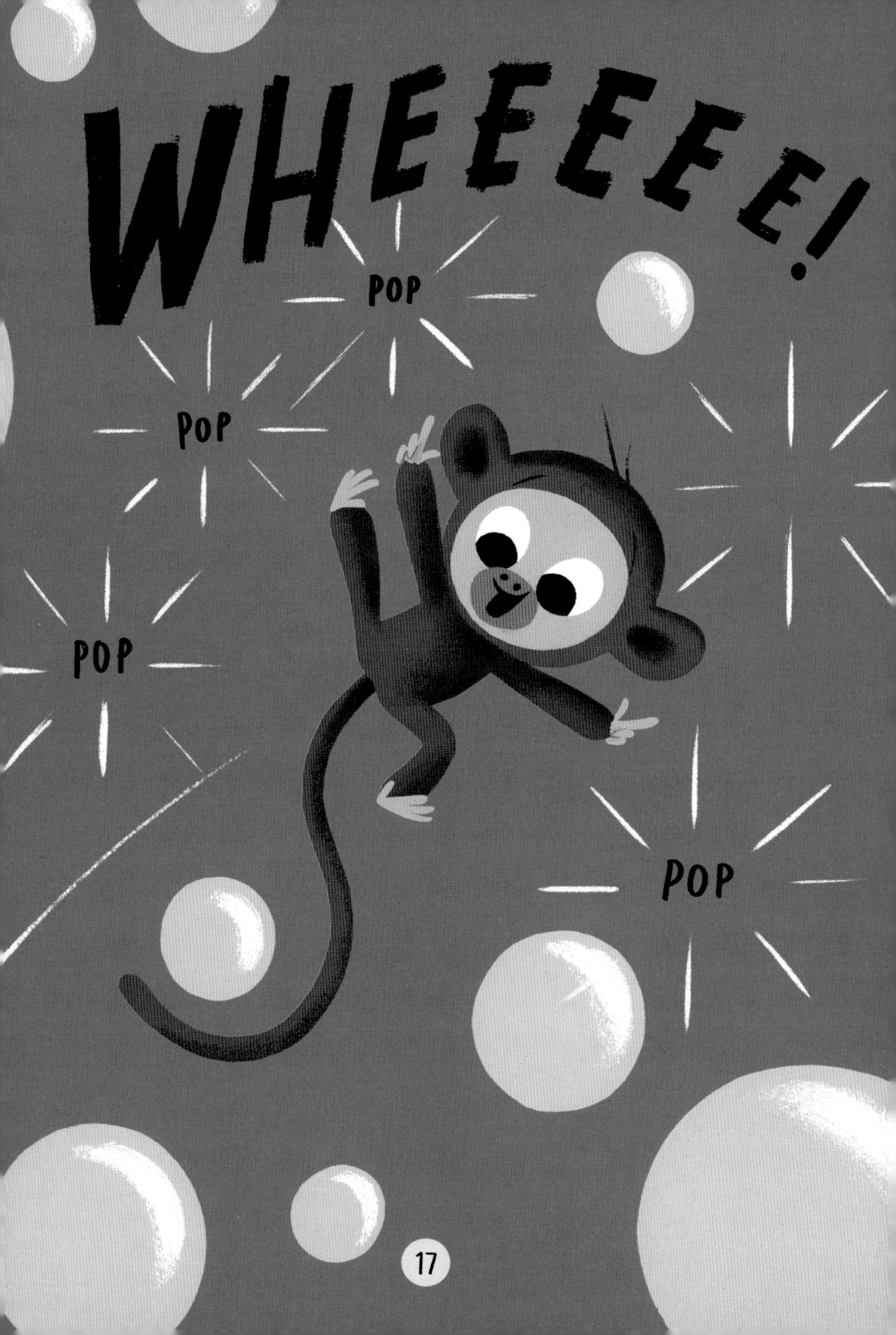
WHEEEEE!
POP
POP
POP
POP

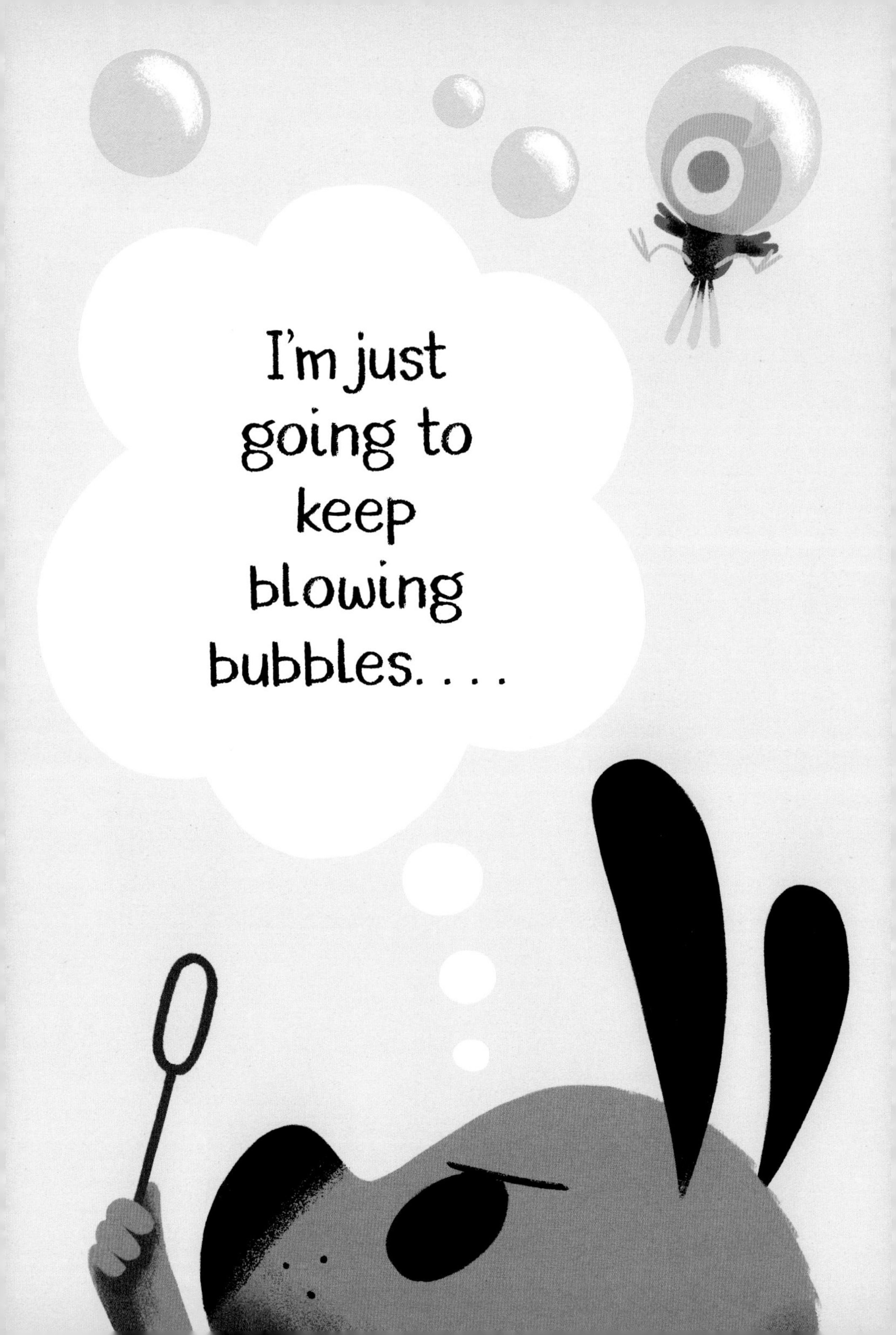
I'm just going to keep blowing bubbles. . . .

I'm just
going to
keep
popping
bubbles....

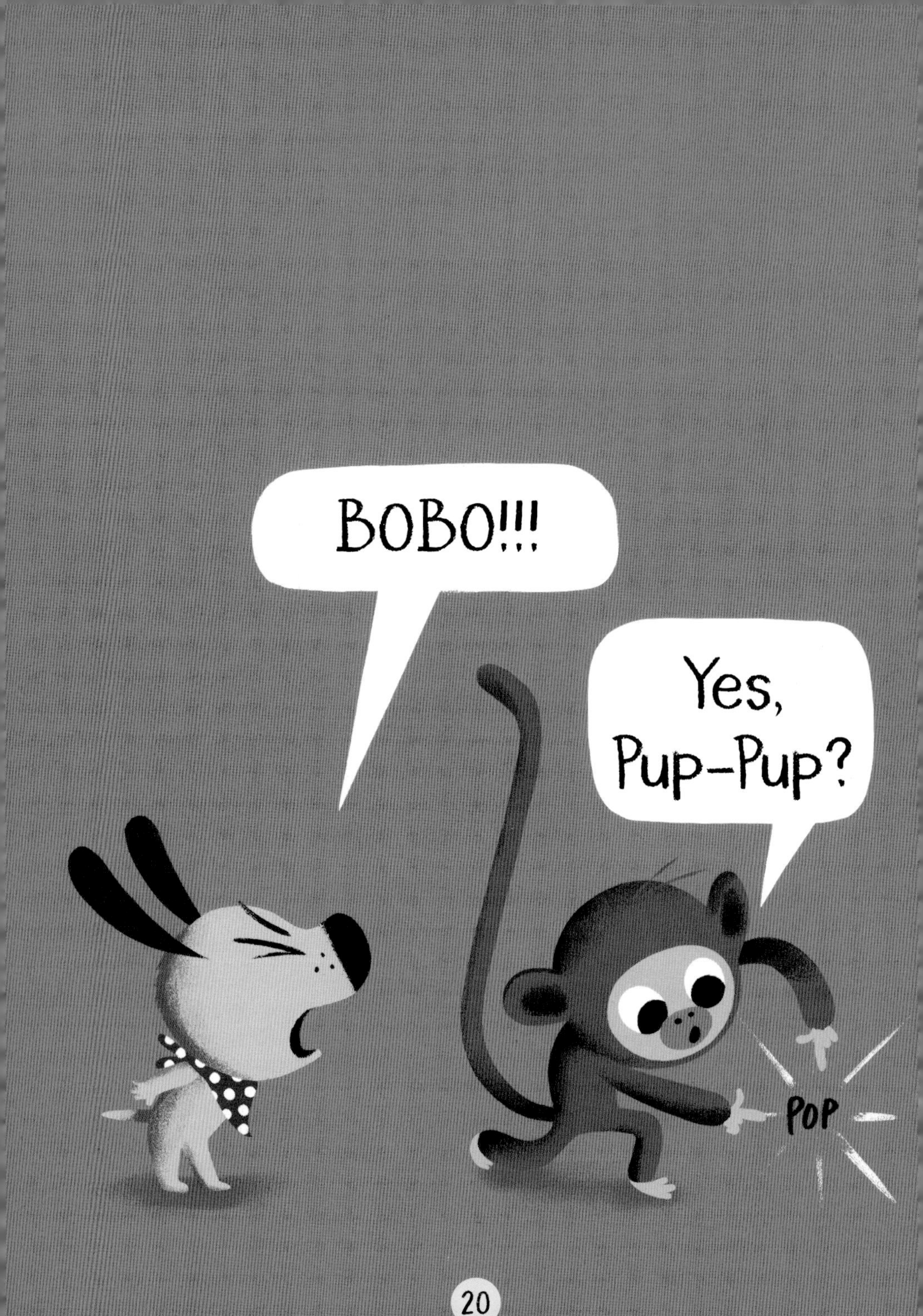
BOBO!!!
Yes, Pup-Pup?
POP

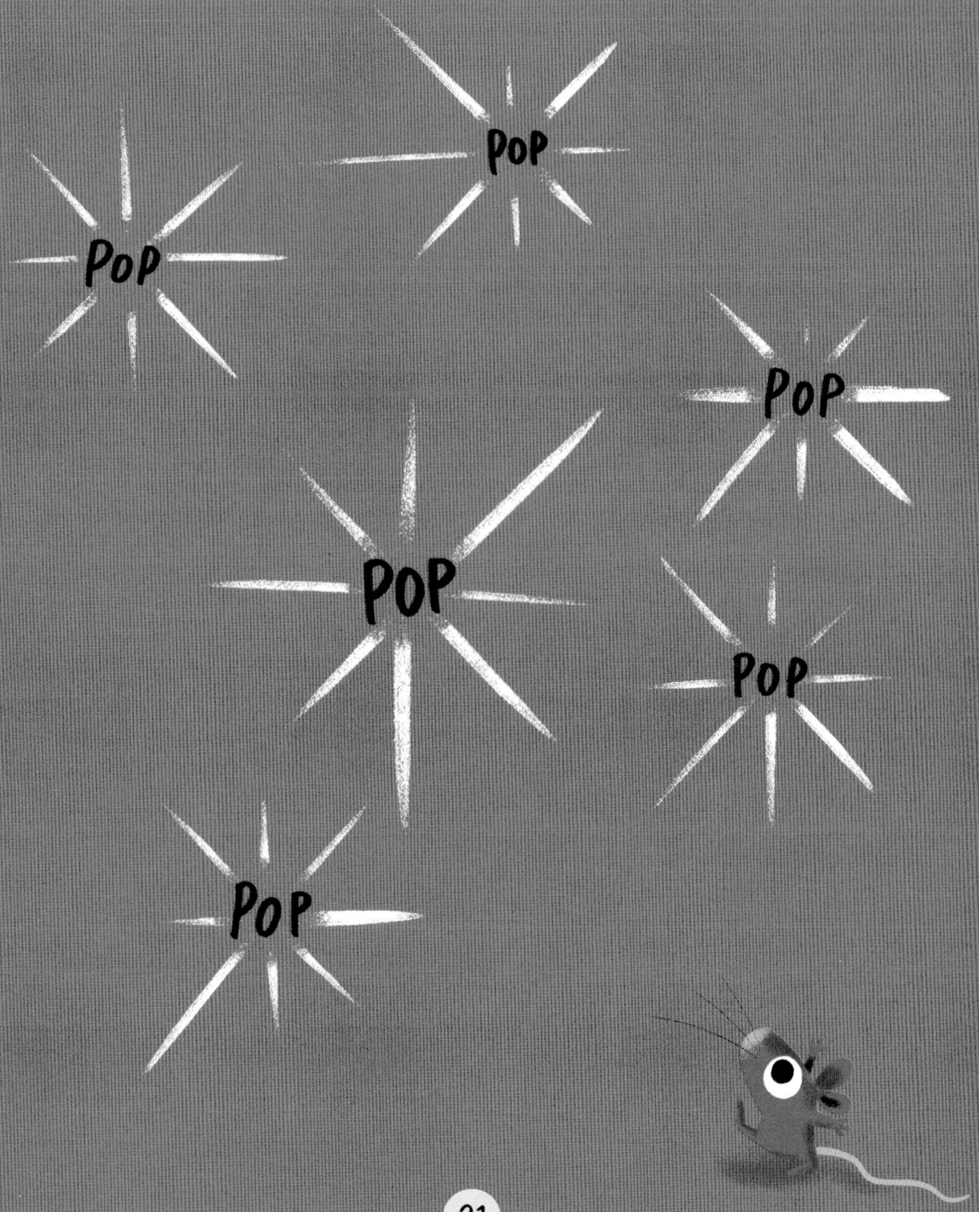
POP
POP
POP
POP
POP
POP

STOP
POPPING MY
BUBBLES!!!

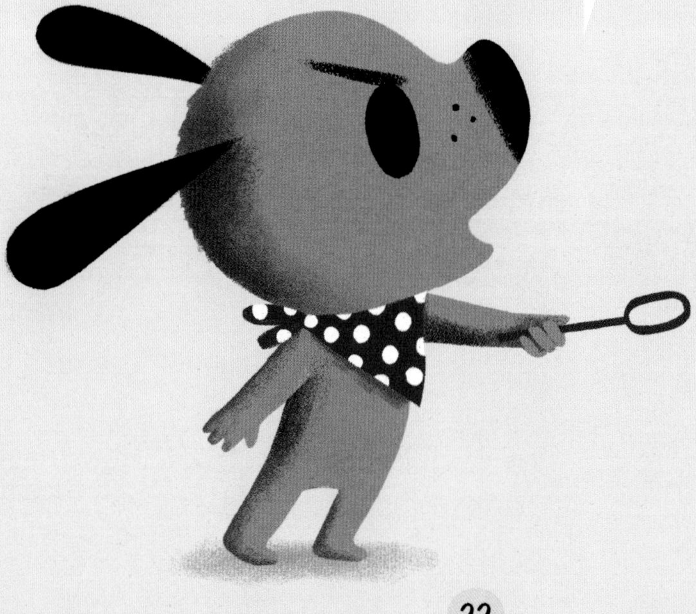

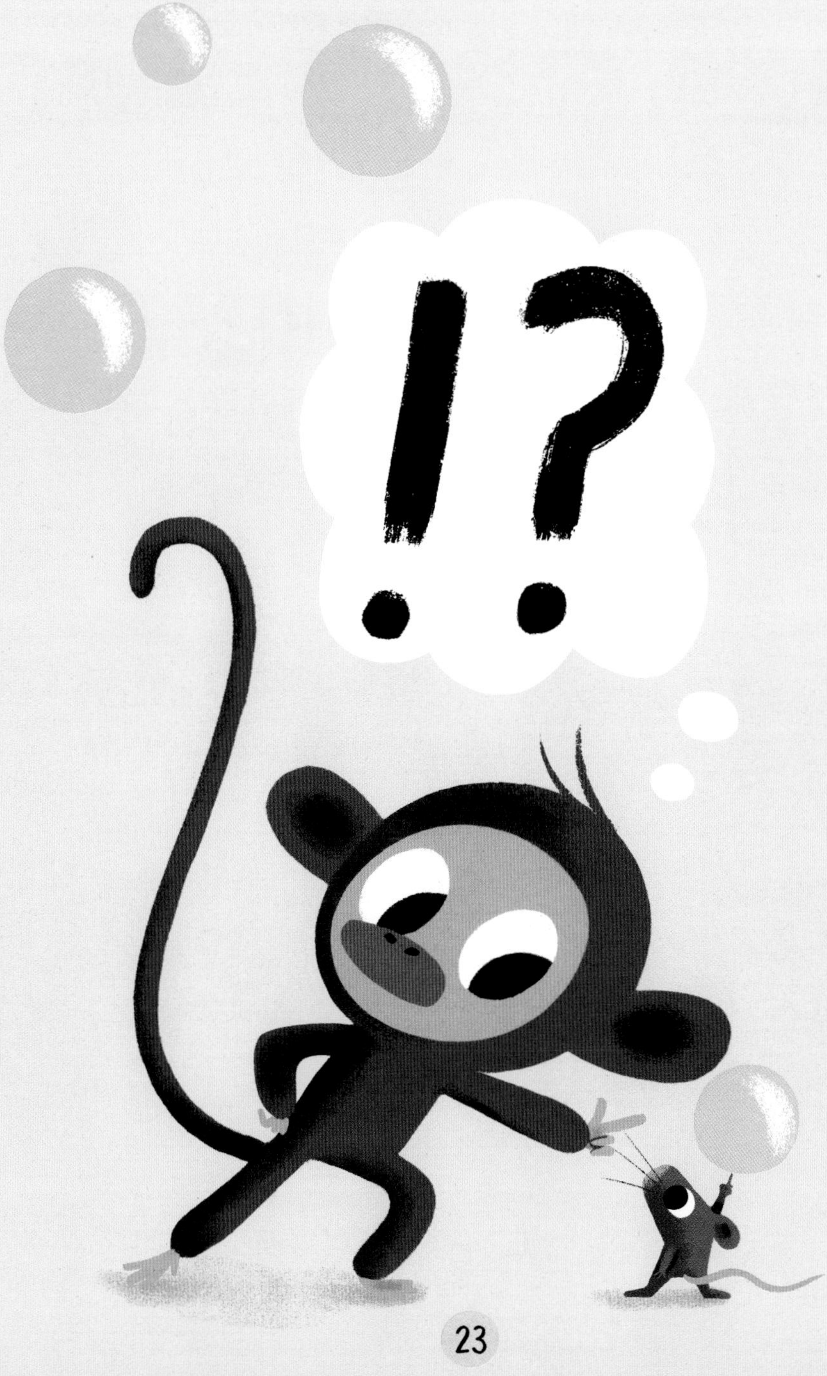
!?

# Chapter 3
# Better Bubbles?

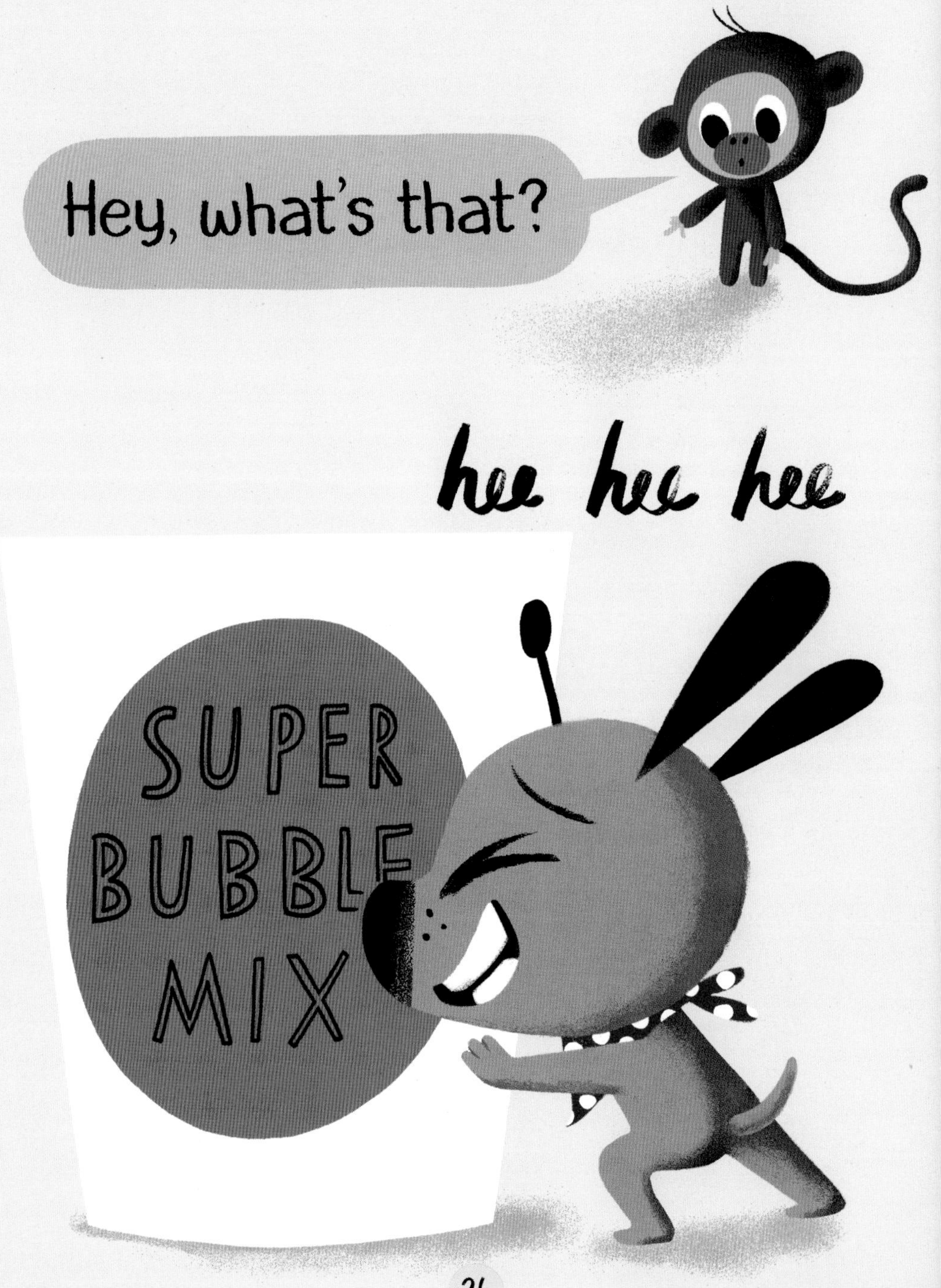
Hey, what's that?
hee hee hee
SUPER
BUBBLE
MIX

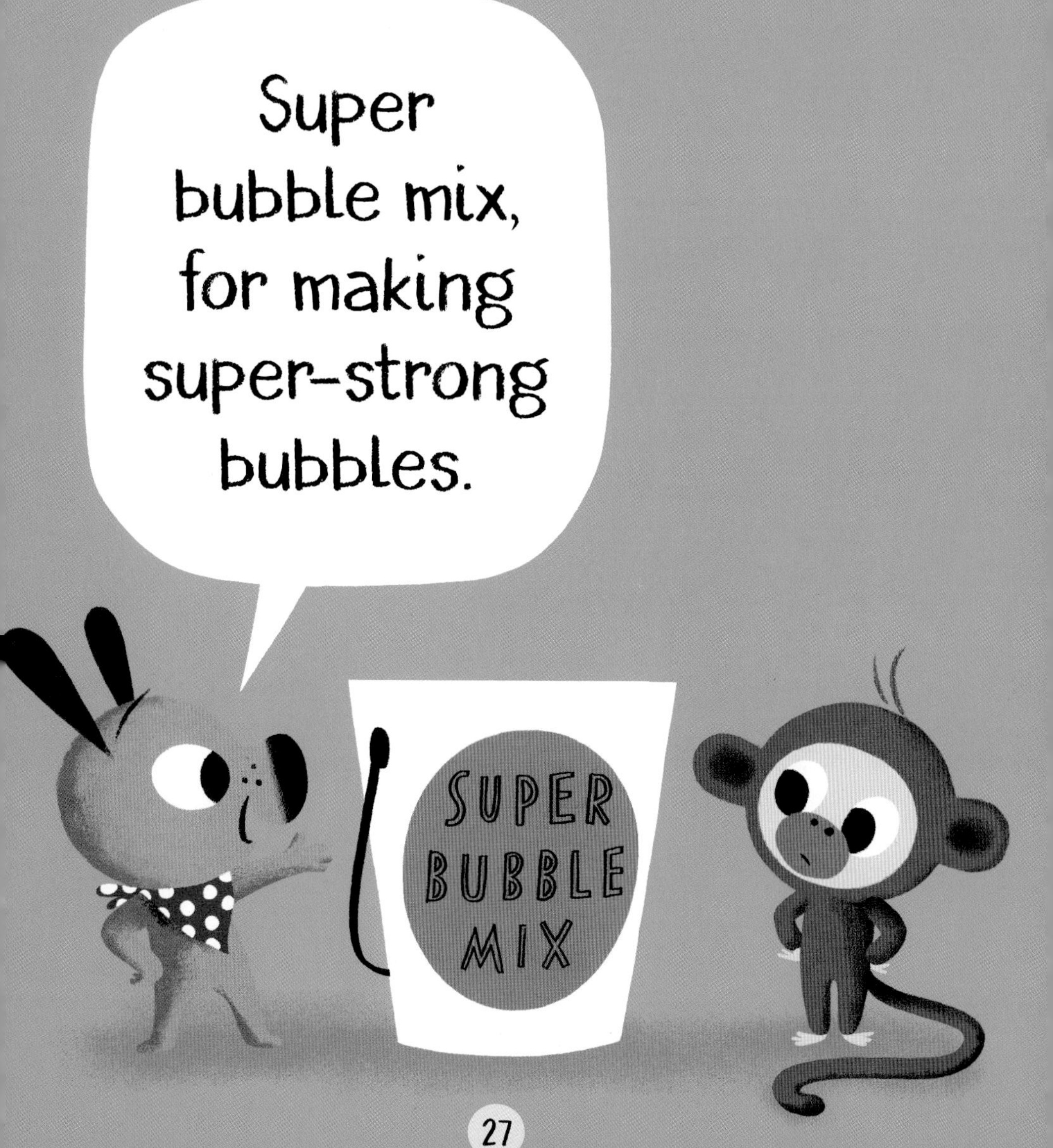
Super bubble mix, for making super-strong bubbles.
SUPER BUBBLE MIX

. . . NO ONE can POP them!

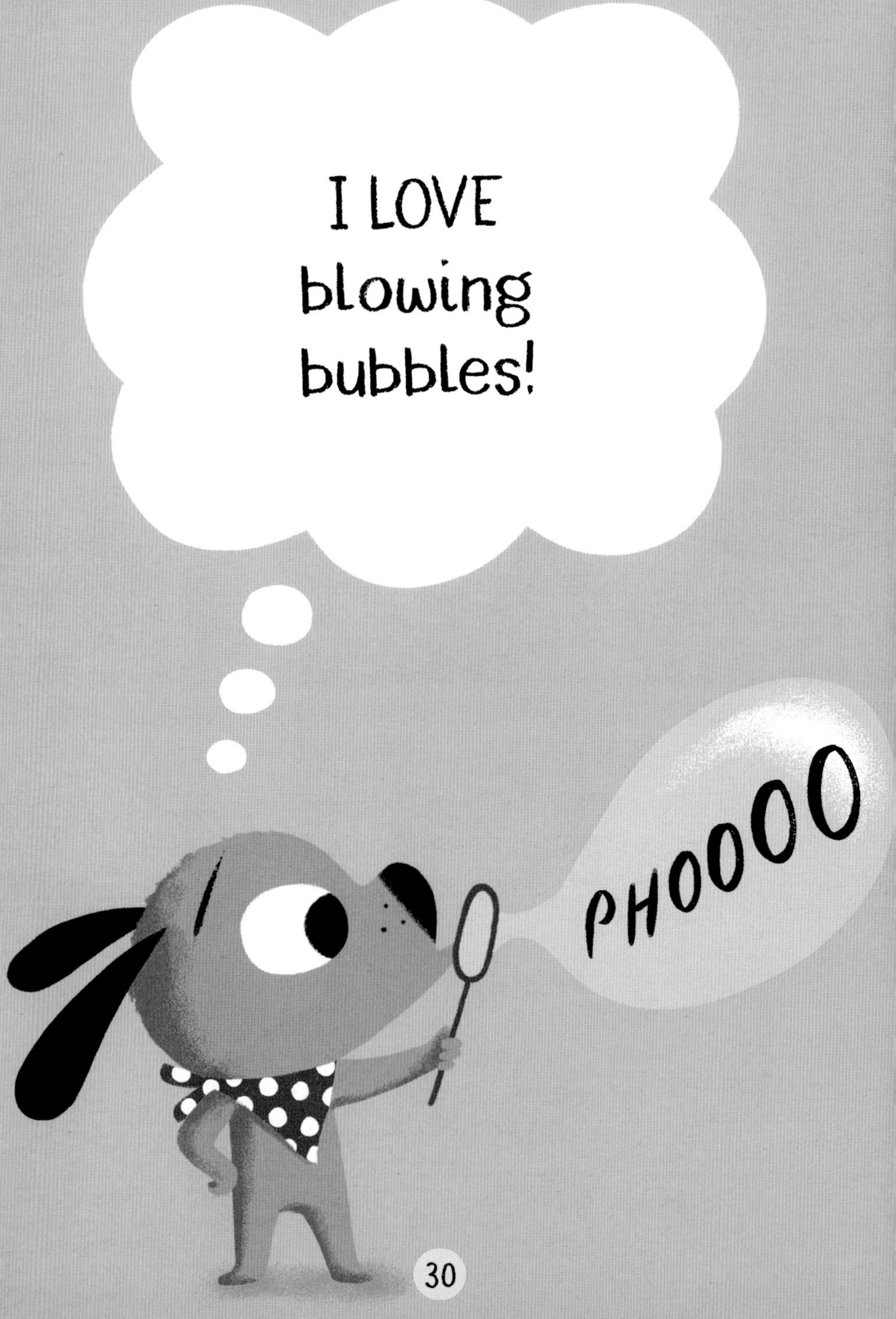
I LOVE
blowing
bubbles!
PHOOOO

I LOVE
popping
bubbles!

hee hee hee

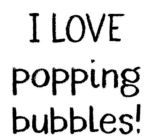

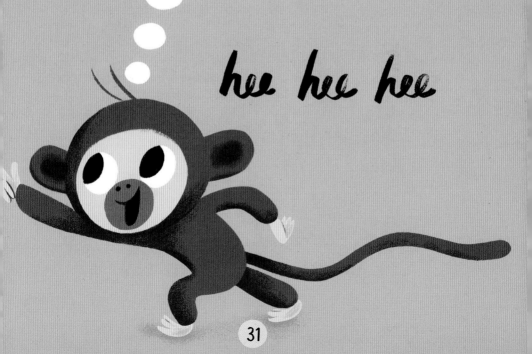

# Chapter 4
# Bubble Trouble!

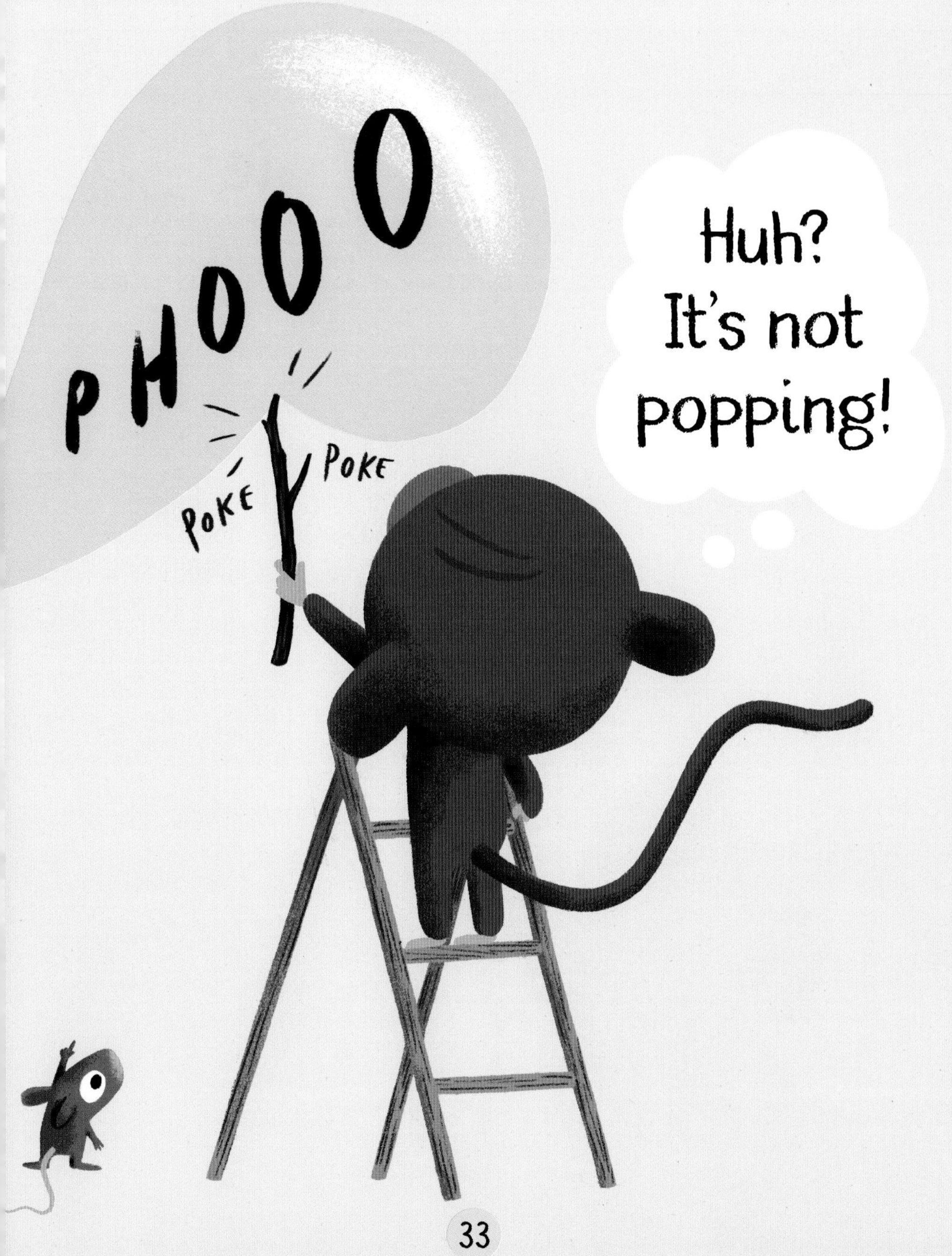
PHOOO
POKE
POKE
Huh?
It's not
popping!

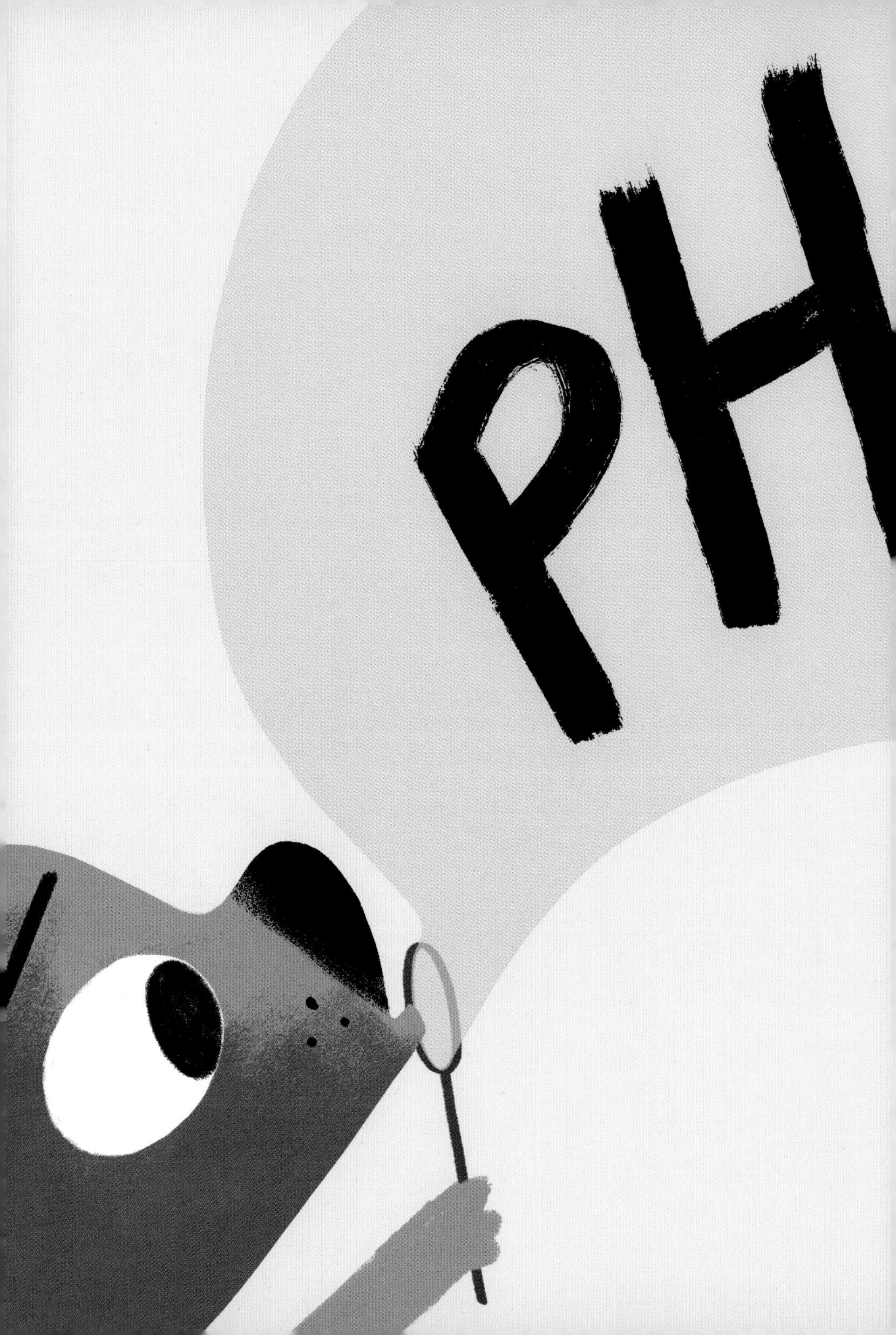
PH

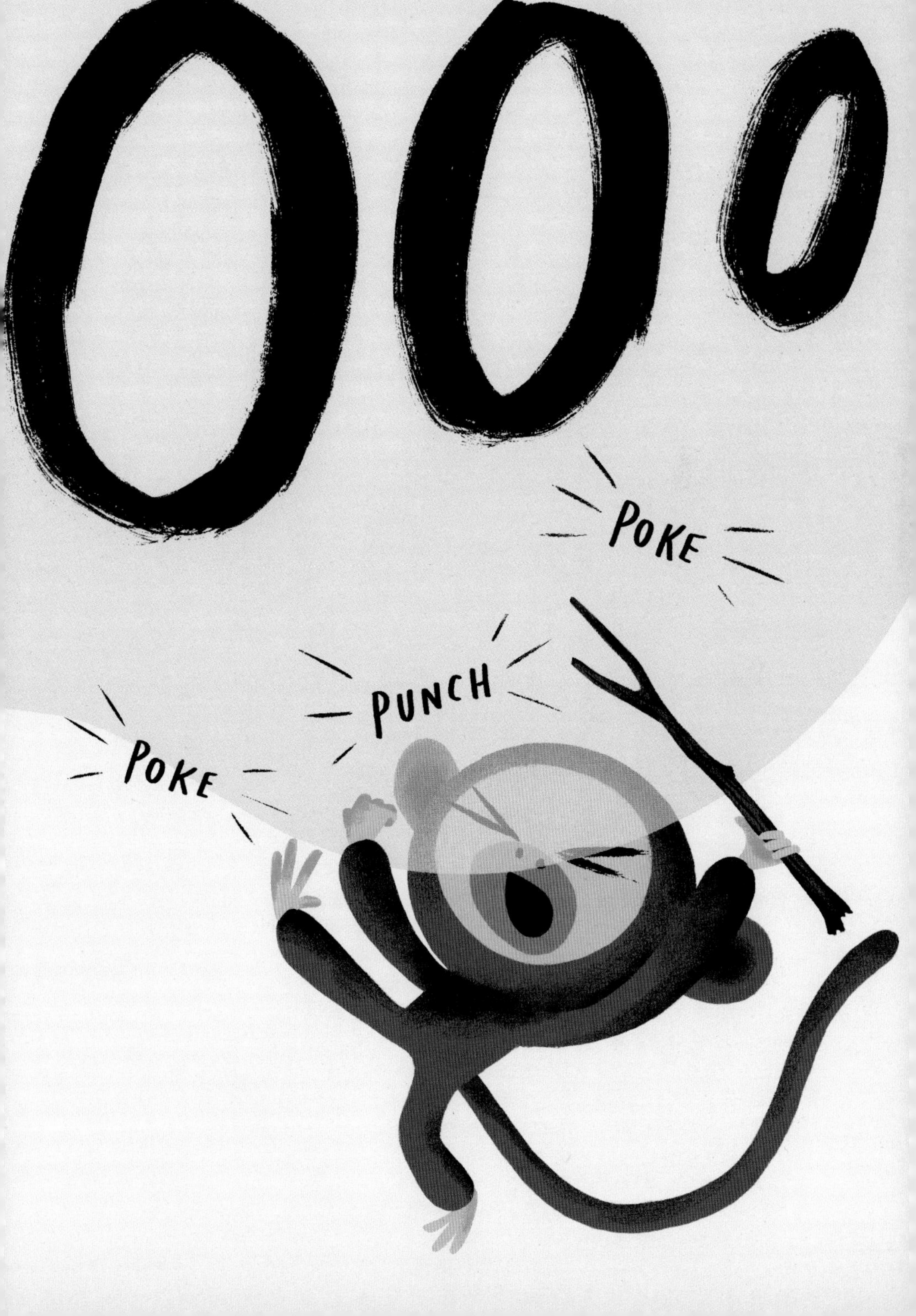
OOo
POKE
PUNCH
POKE

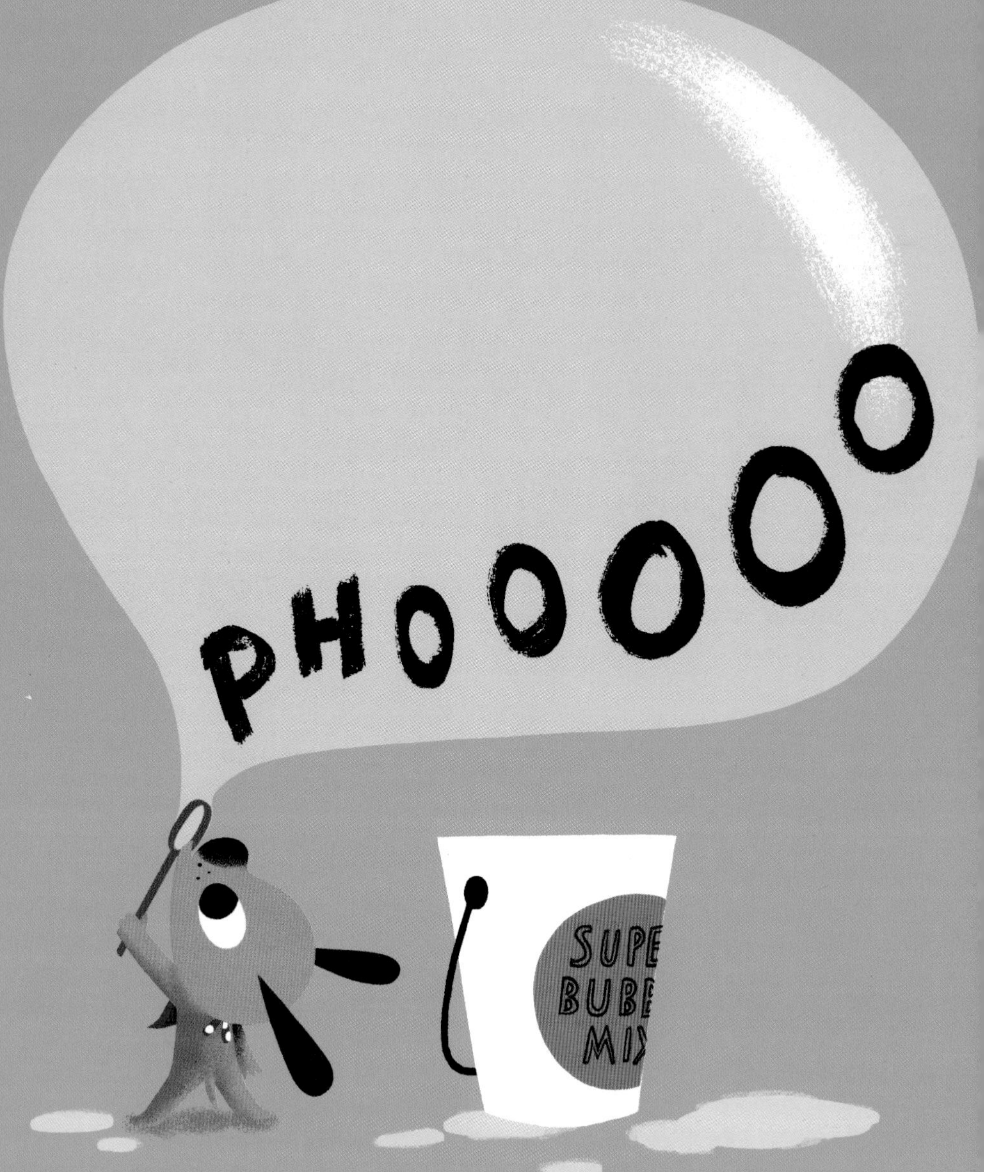
PHOOOOOO
SUPE
BUBB
MIX

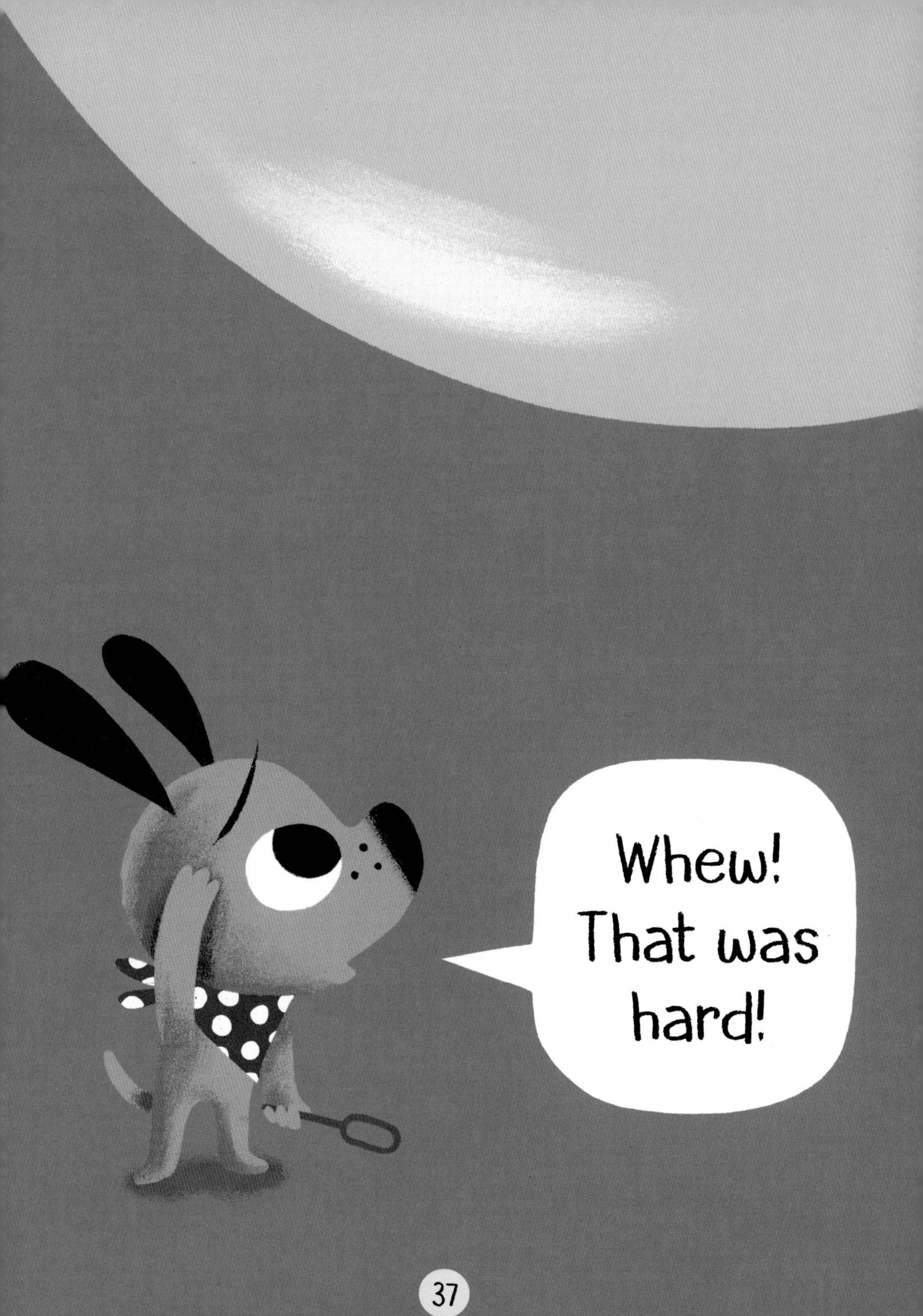
Whew! That was hard!

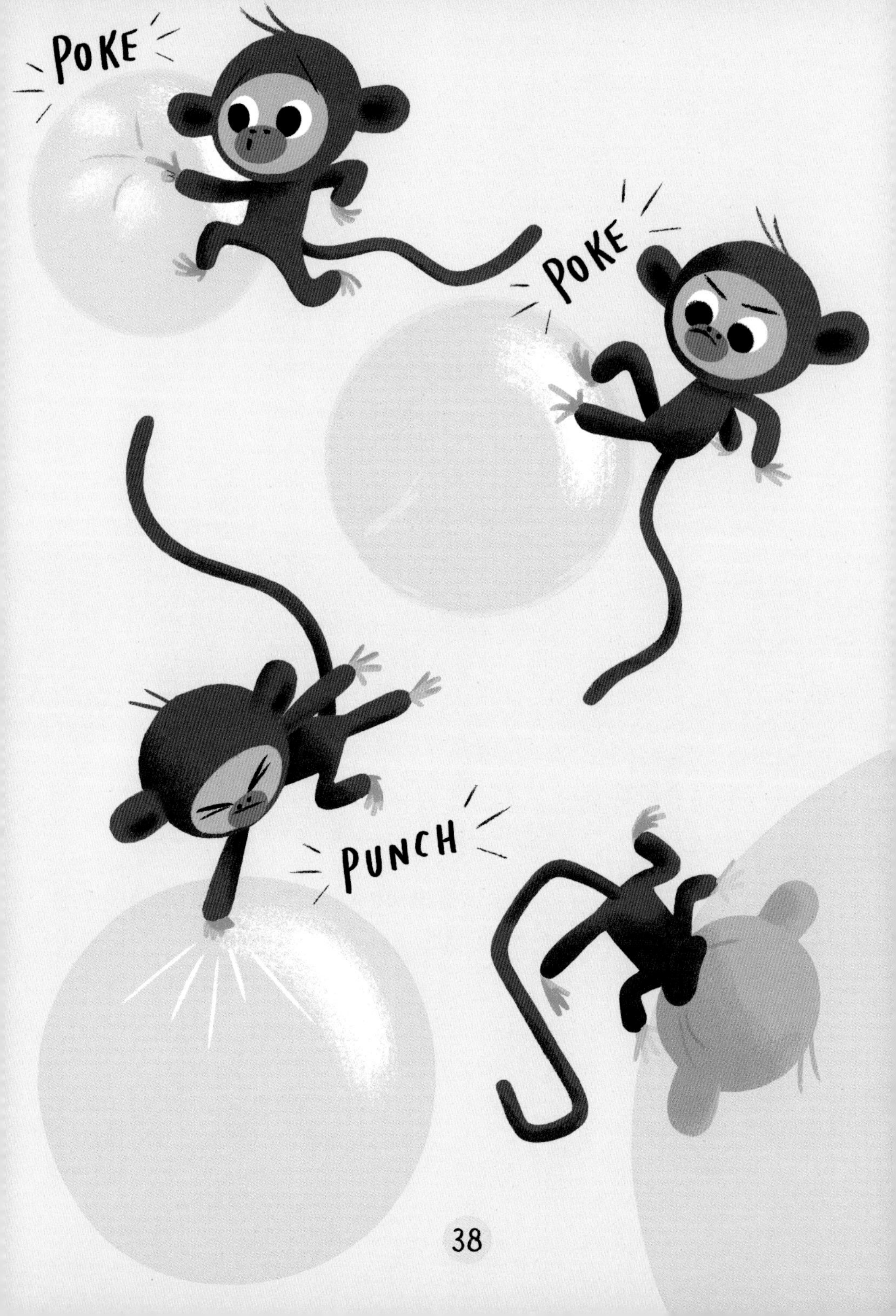
POKE
POKE
PUNCH

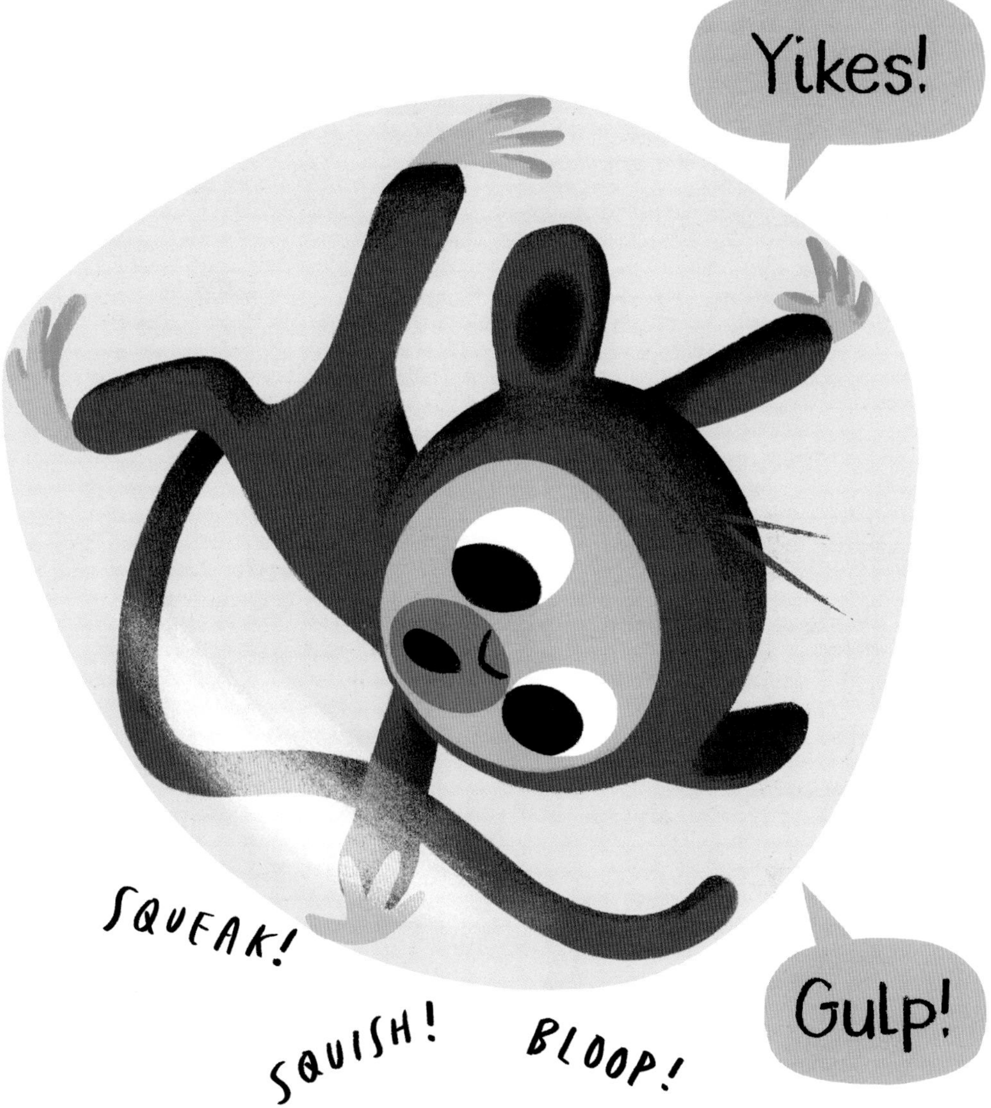
Yikes!
SQUEAK!
SQUISH!
BLOOP!
Gulp!

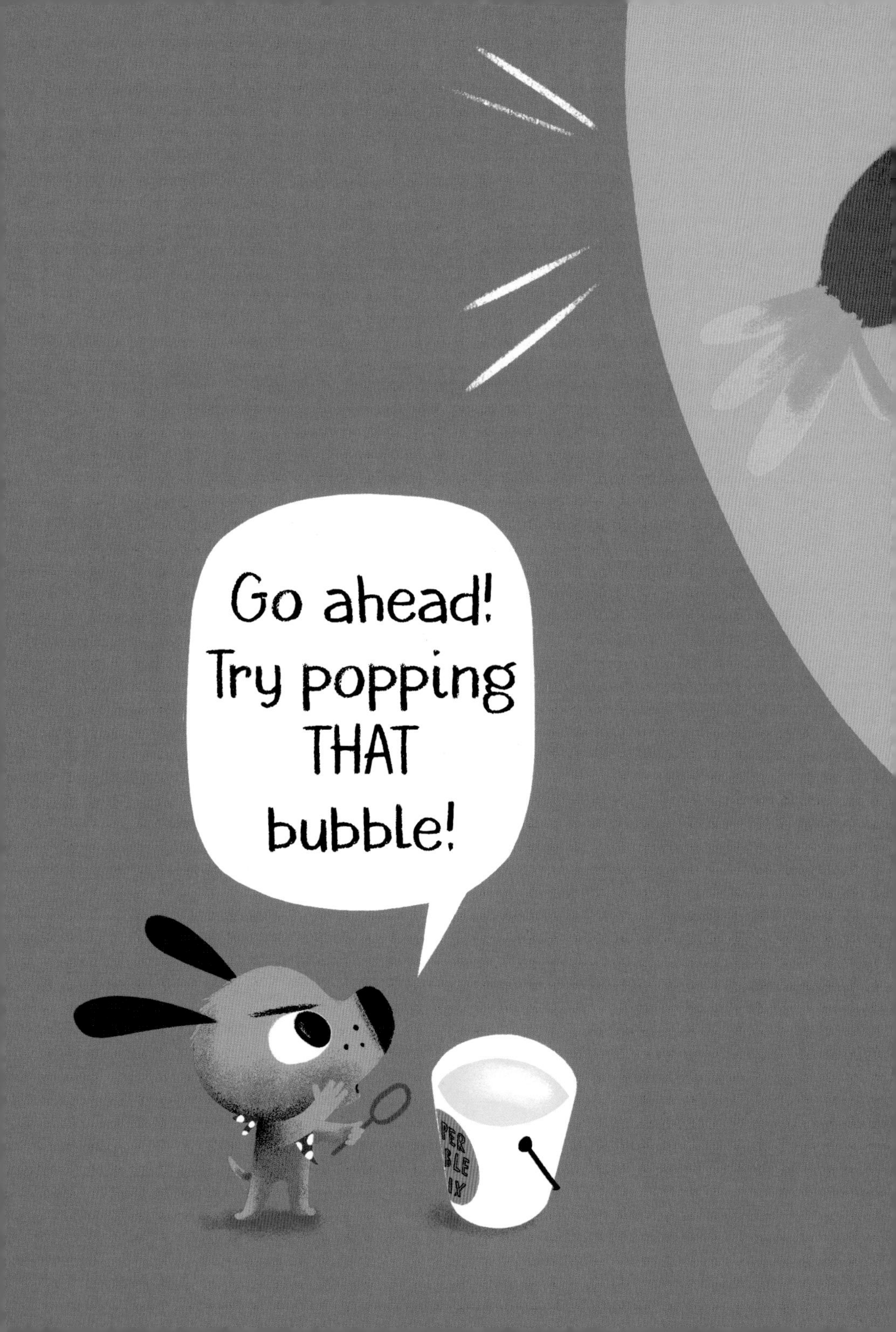
Go ahead! Try popping THAT bubble!

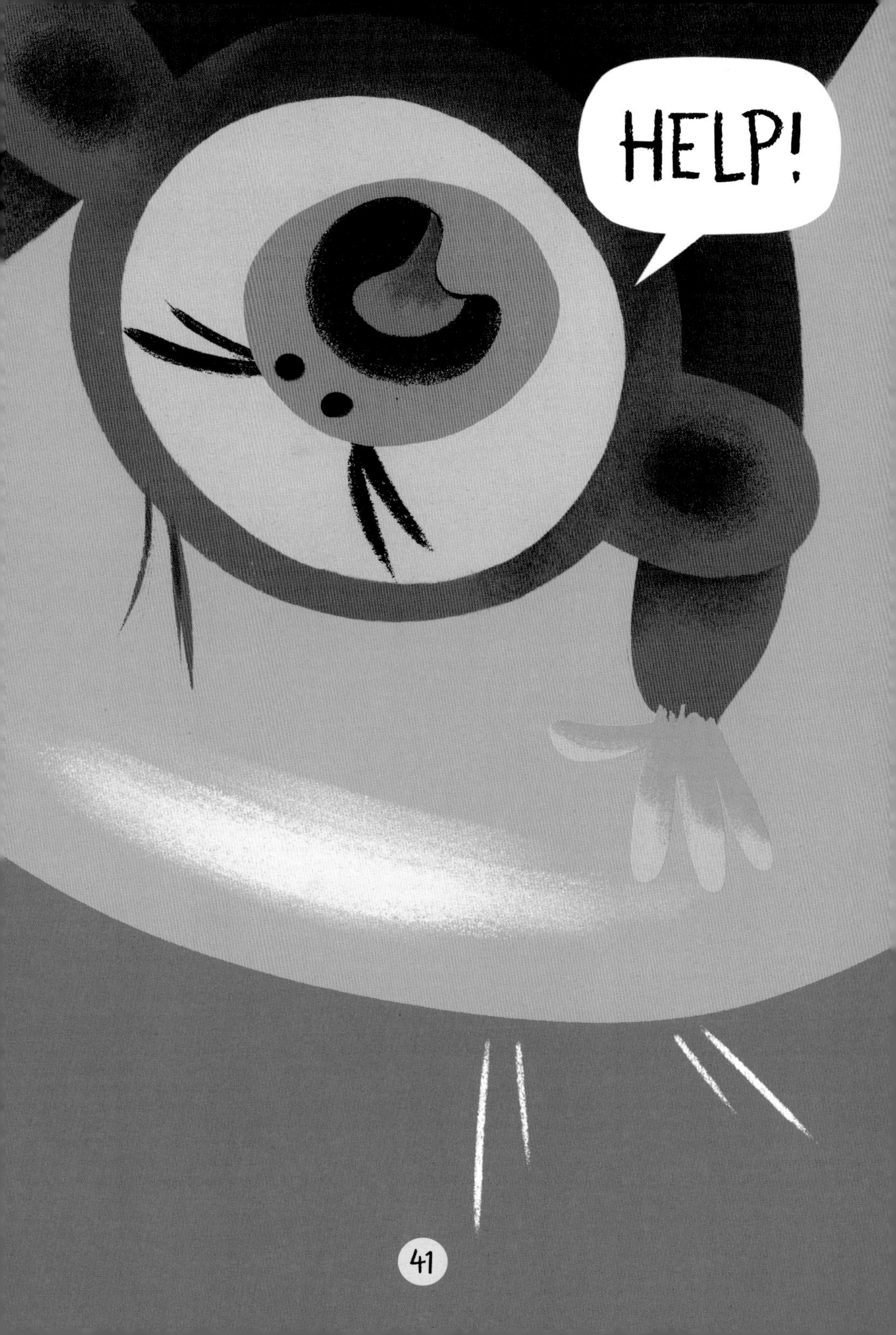
HELP!

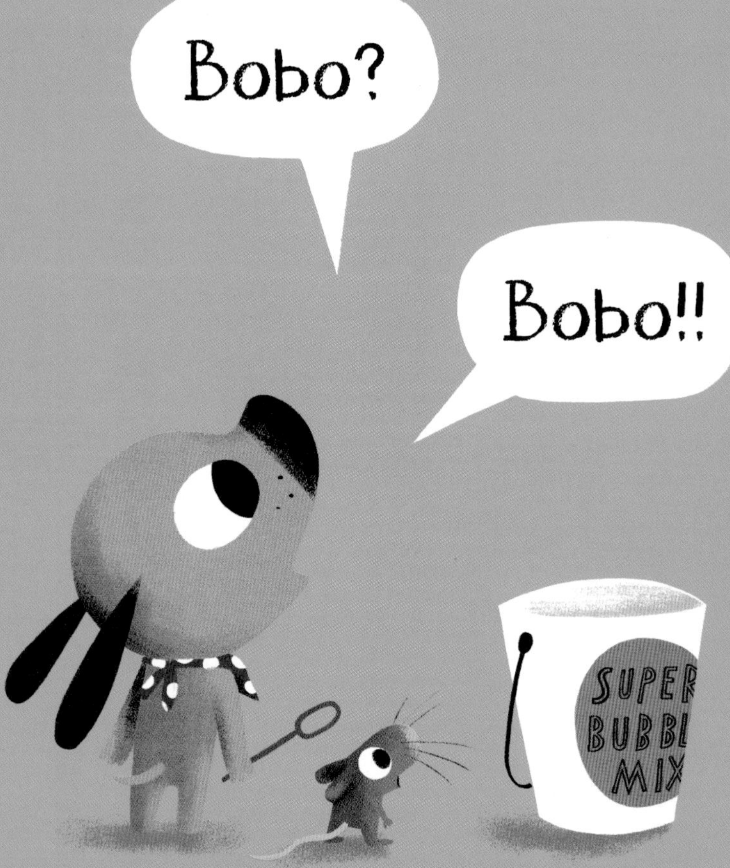
Bobo?
Bobo!!
SUPER
MIX

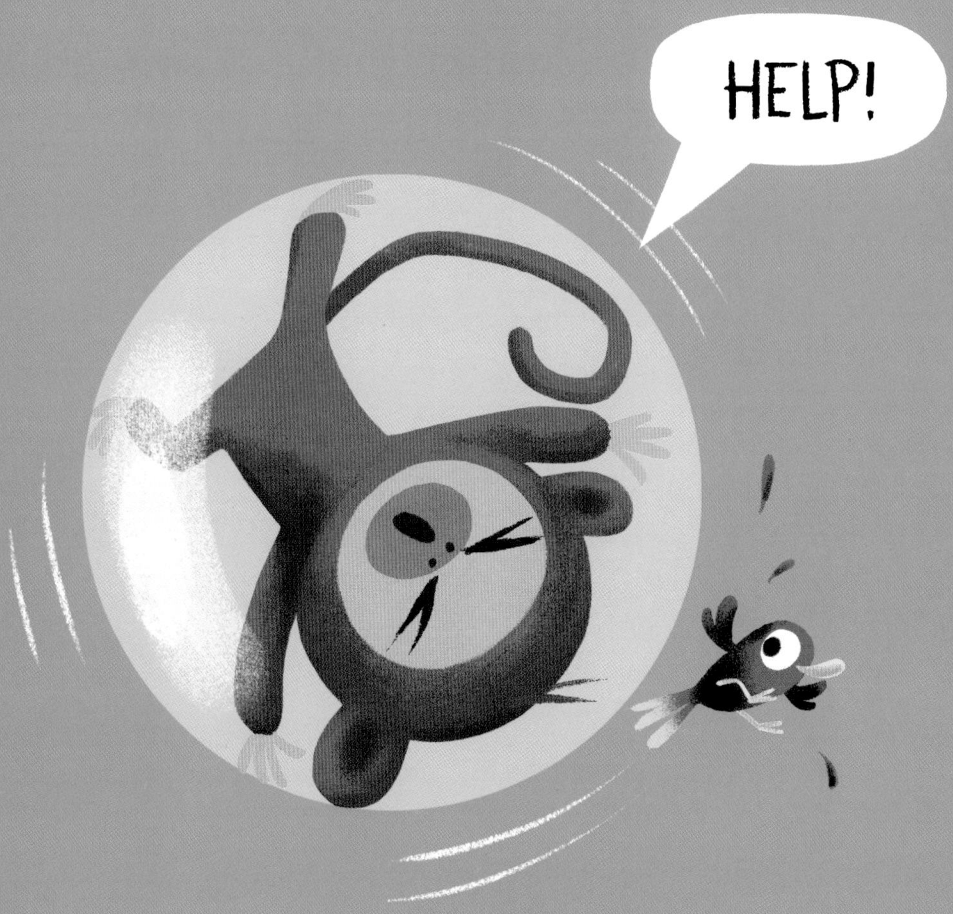
HELP!

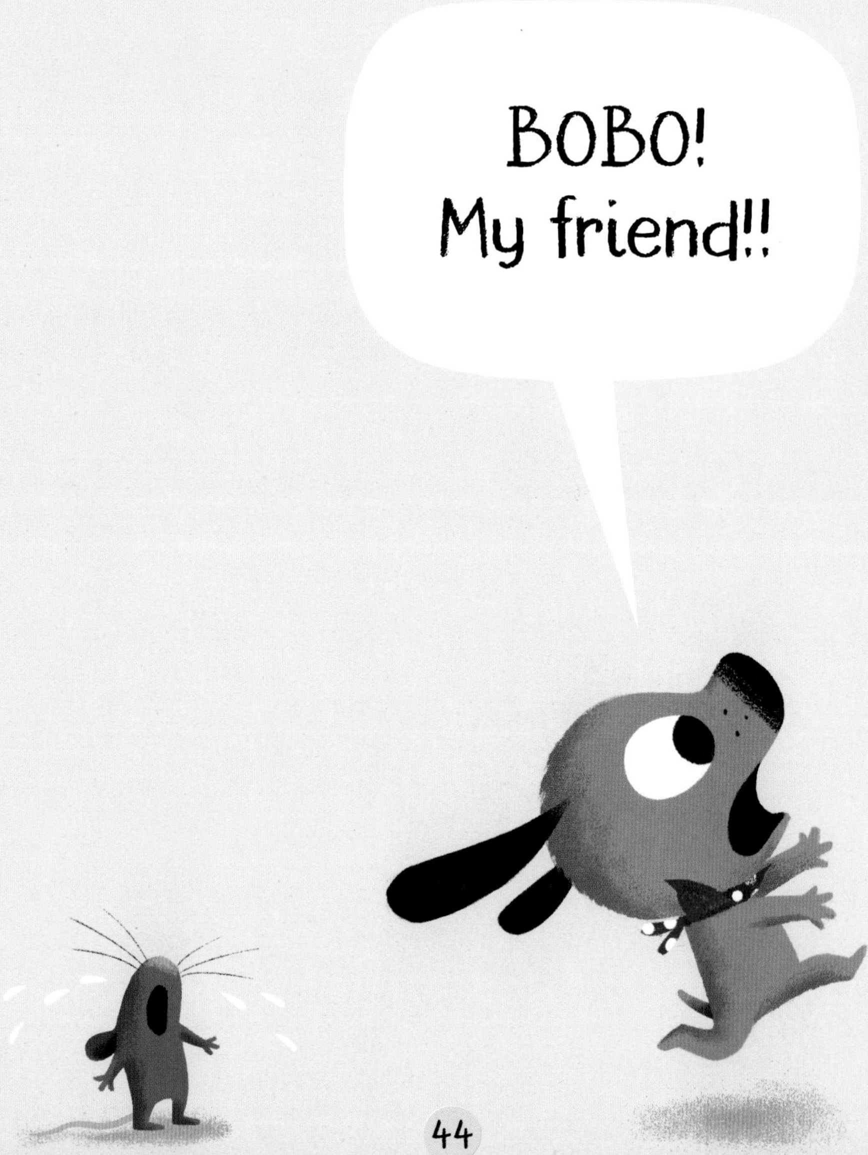
BOBO! My friend!!

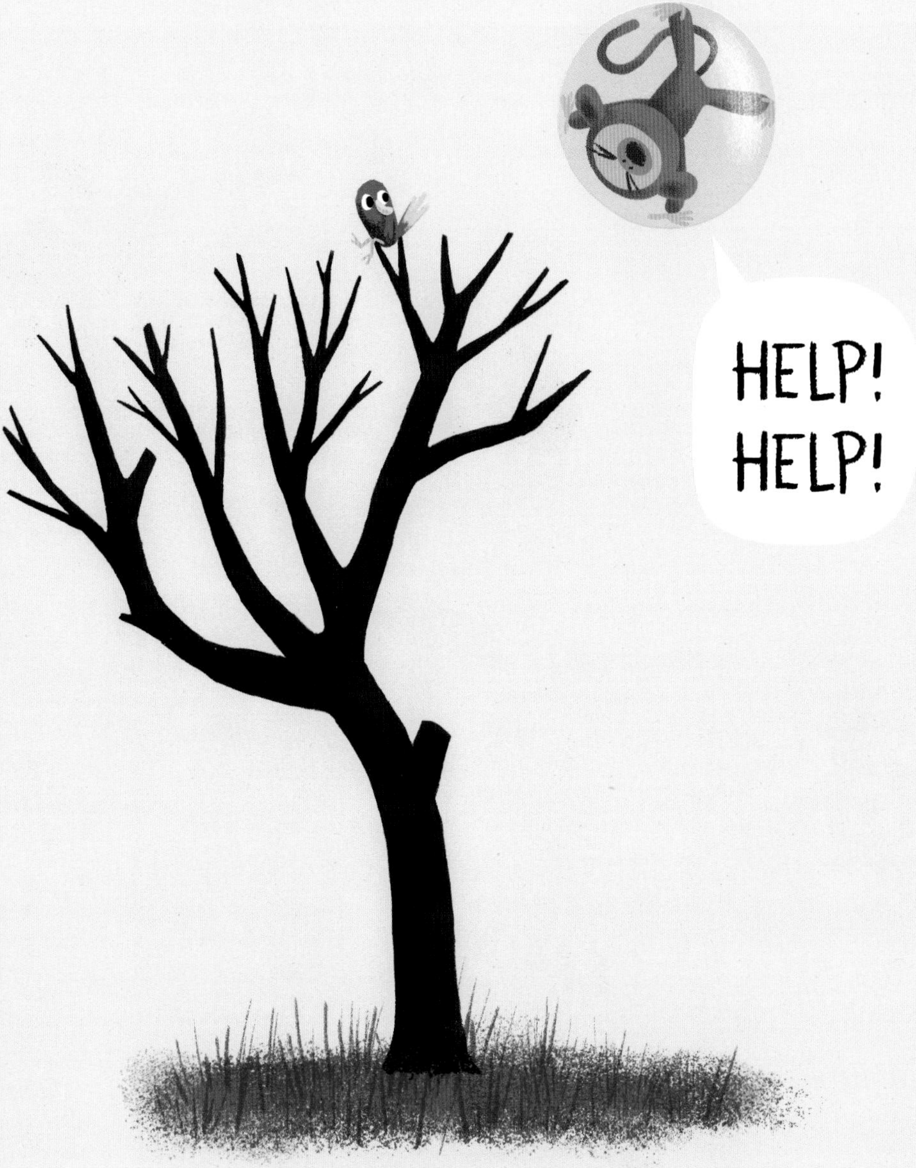
HELP! HELP!

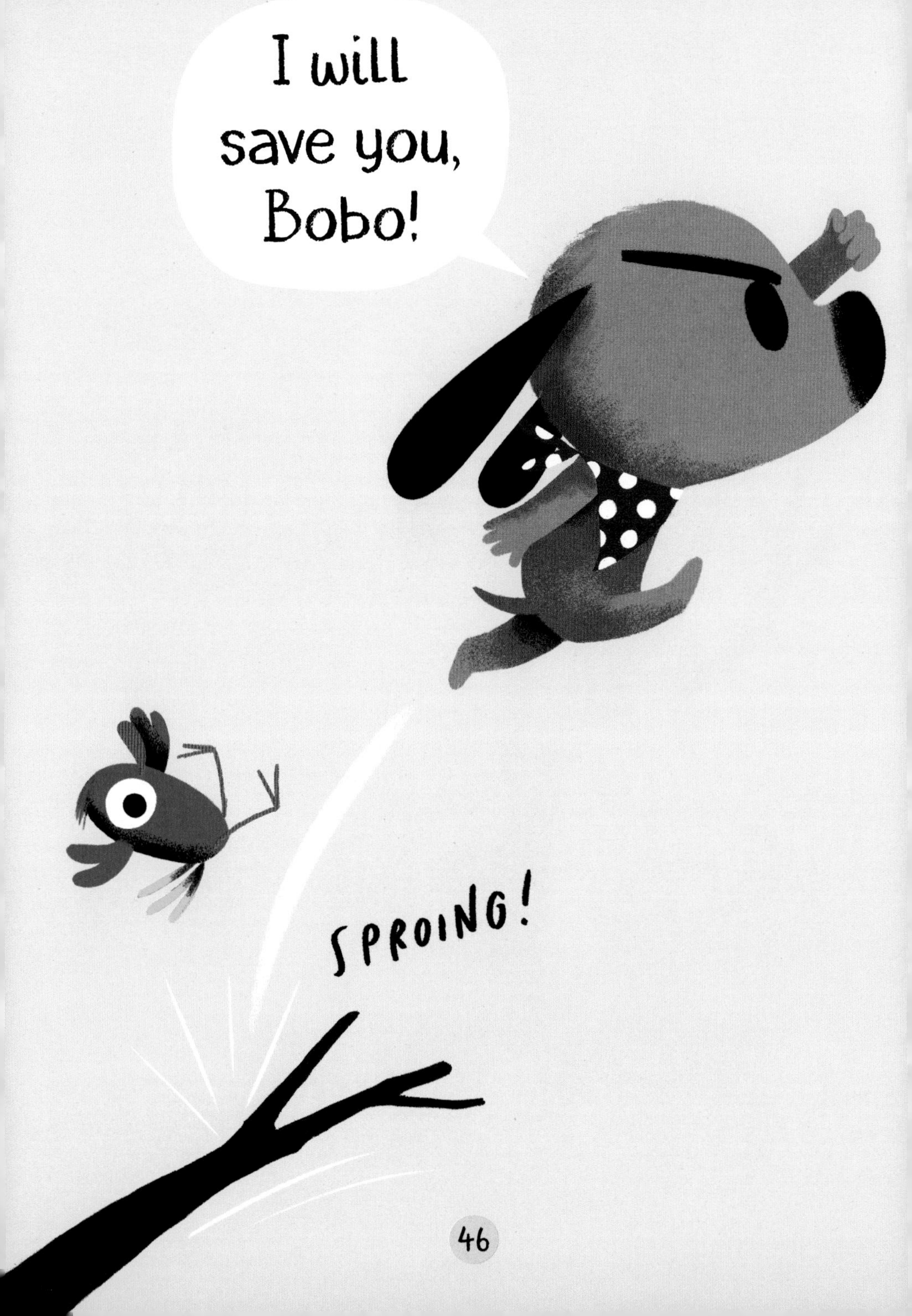
I will save you, Bobo!
SPROING!

Save me,
Pup-Pup!
Save me!

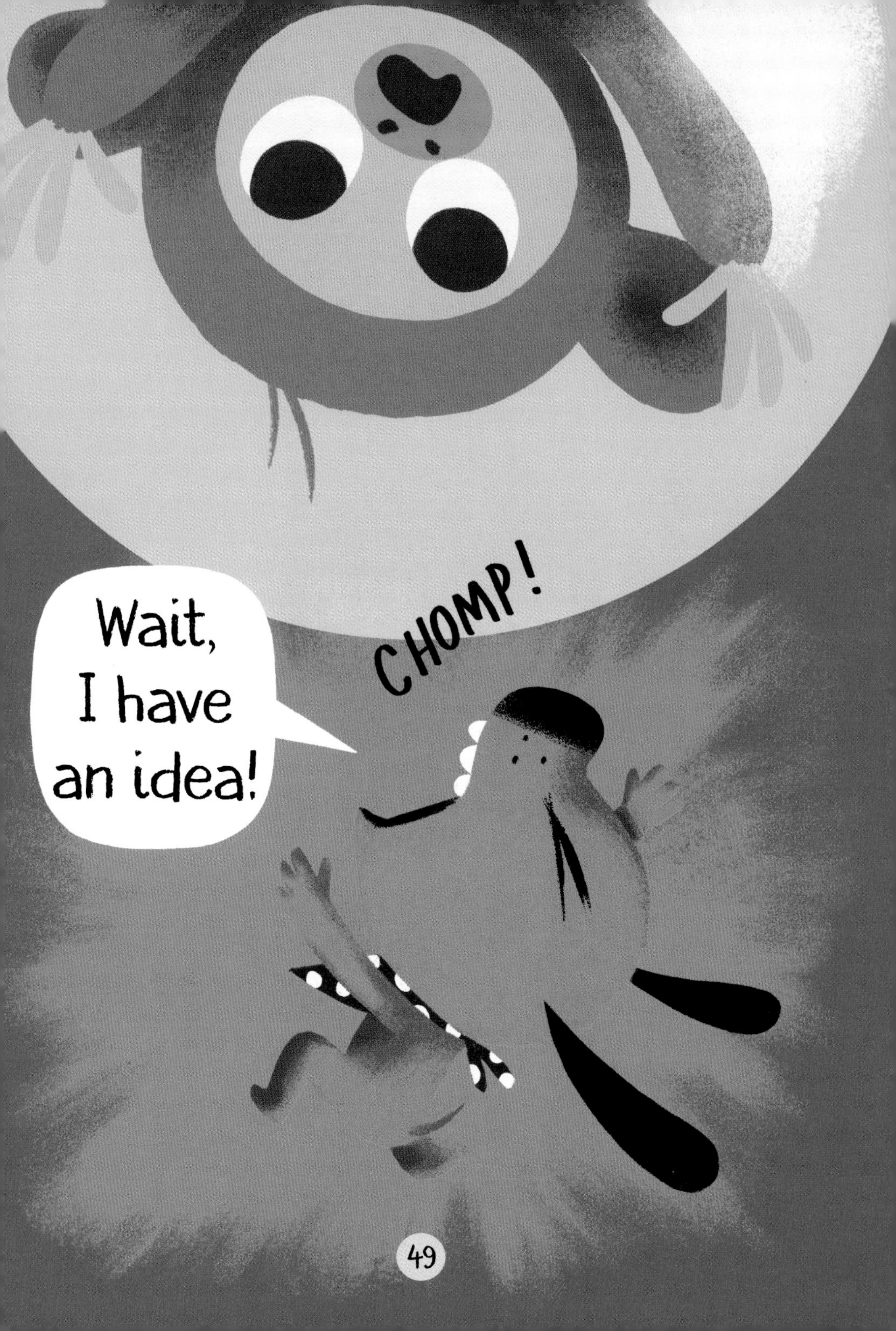
Wait, I have an idea!
CHOMP!

# Chapter 5
## Burst My Bubble

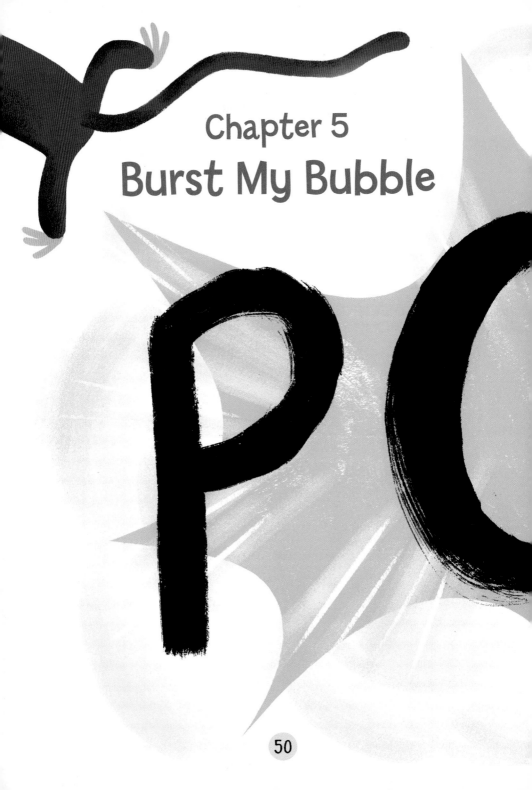

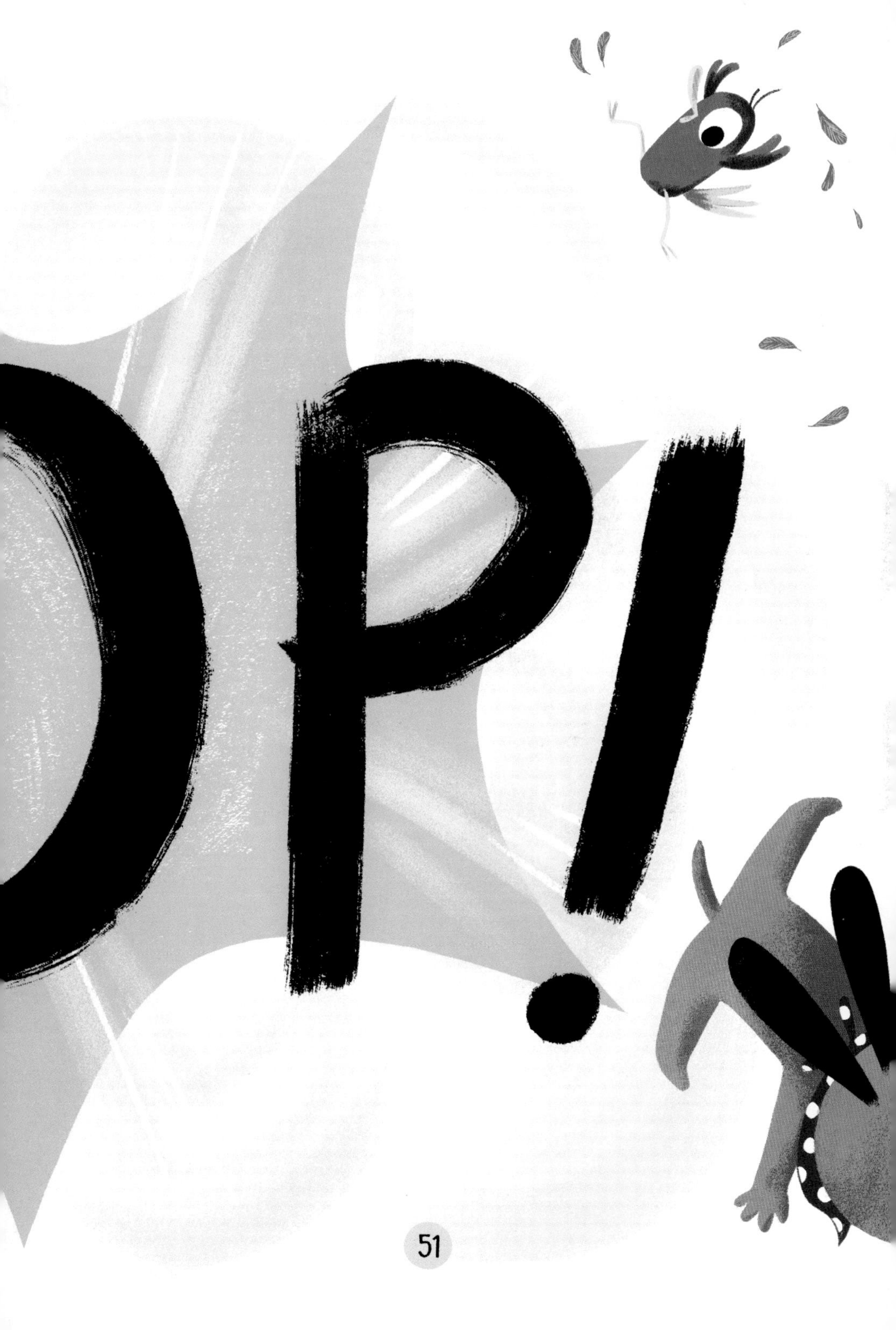
OP!

bubble soap mix
SUPER BUBBLE MIX

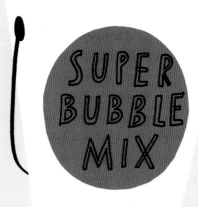

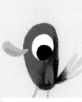

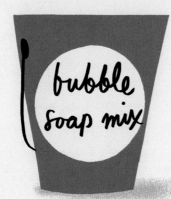

# Chapter 6
# We Still Love Bubbles!

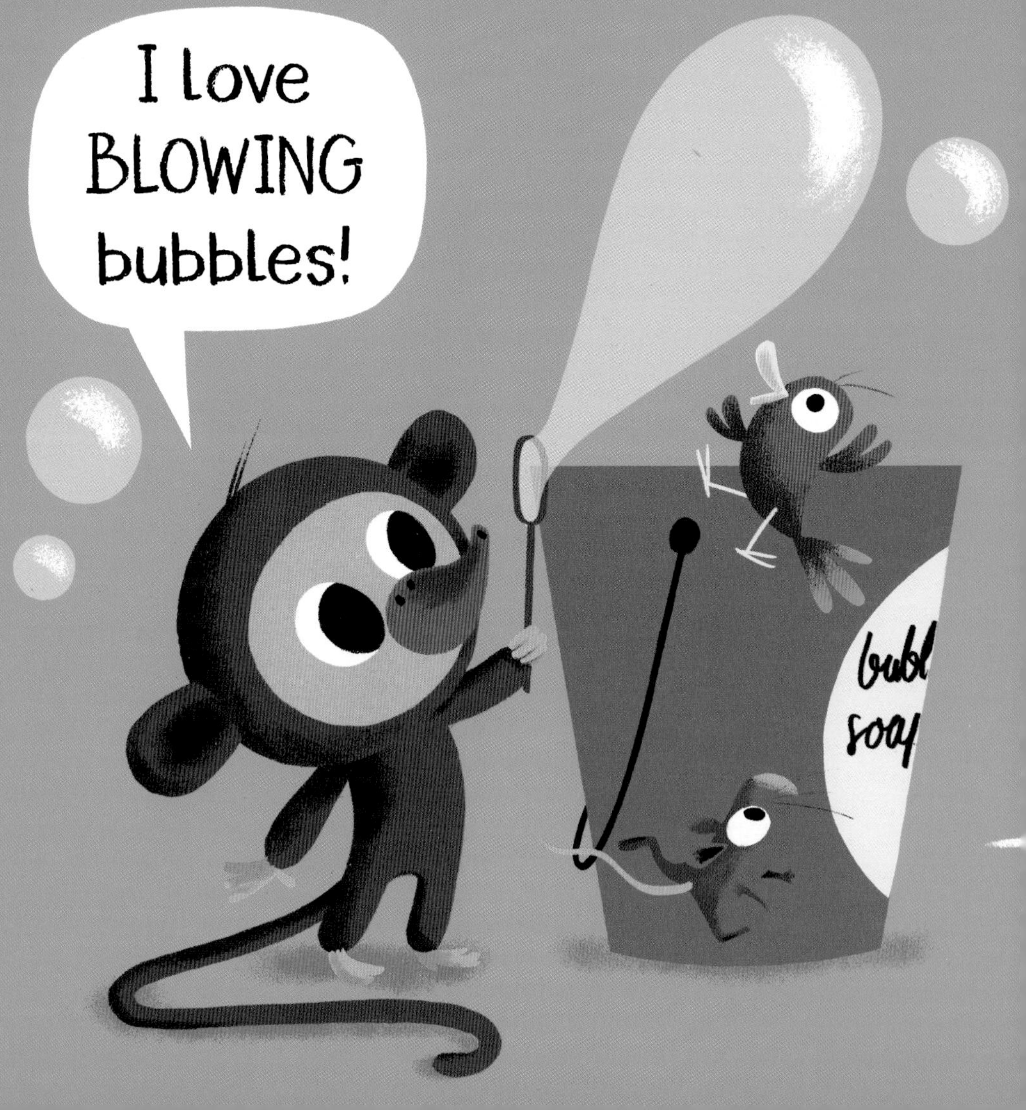
I love BLOWING bubbles!

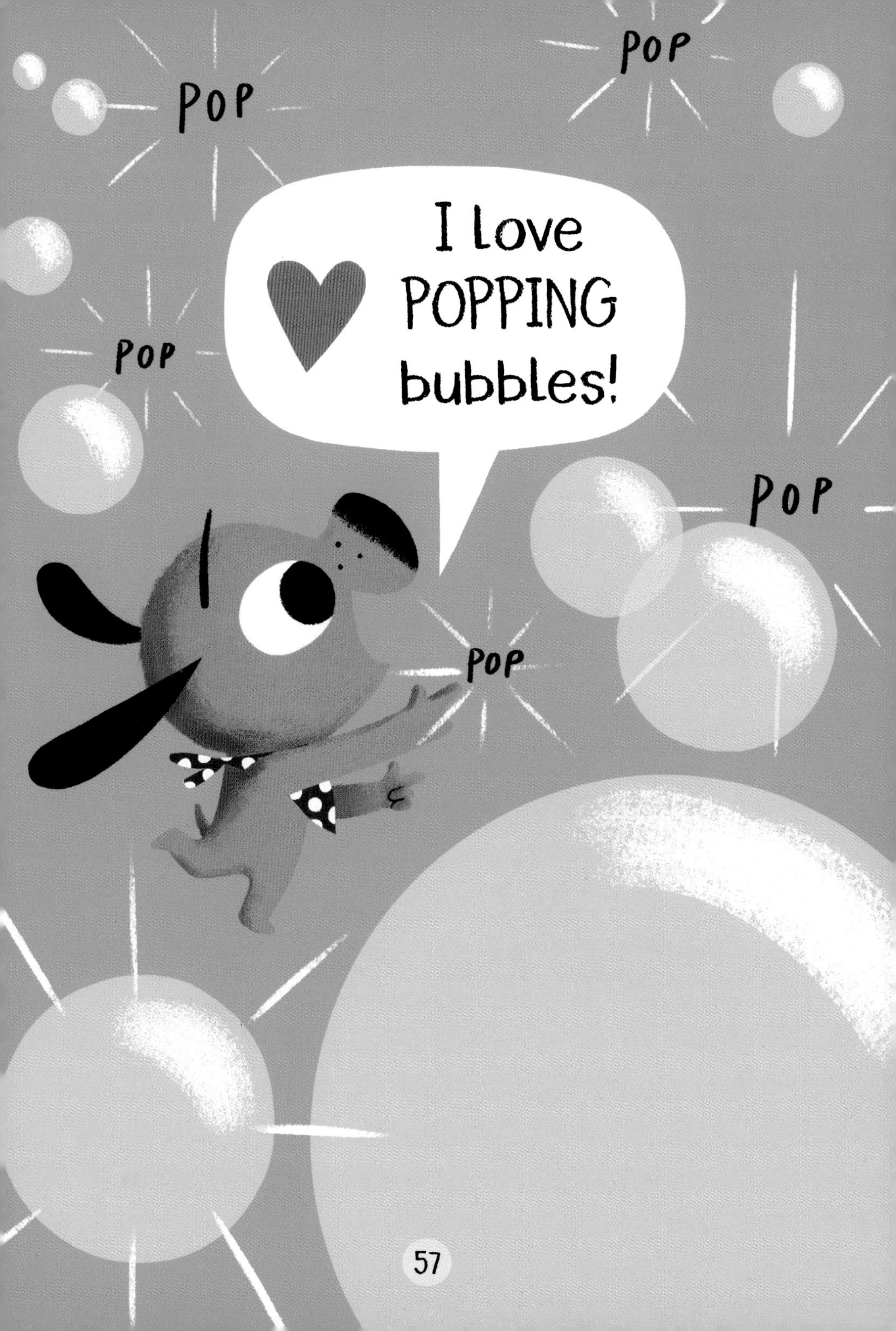
POP
POP
I love POPPING bubbles!
POP
POP
POP

Hungry for another Bobo and Pup-Pup book?

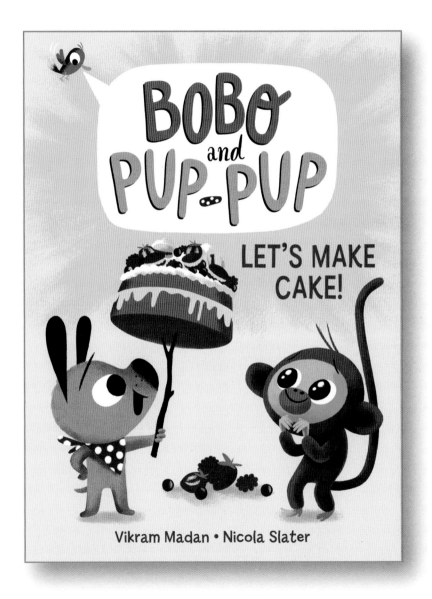

# AWESOME COMICS FOR AWESOME KIDS

Mika Song
DONUT FEED THE
SQUIRRELS

DONUT FEED THE SQUIRRELS

**What will these squirrels do for the chance to eat the perfect donut?**

SHARK AND BOT
Brian Yanish

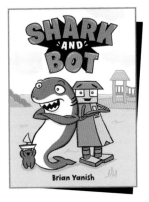

SHARK AND BOT

**Will this mismatched pair become best friends forever?**

Pizza and Taco
WHO'S THE BEST?
STEPHEN SHASKAN

PIZZA AND TACO

**Who's the best?
Find out with food, friends, and waterslides.**

CRABAPPLE TROUBLE
Kaeti Vandorn

CRABAPPLE TROUBLE

**Join Calla and Thistle as they face their fears in this magical adventure!**

RH GRAPHIC

**VISIT US AT RHKIDSGRAPHIC.COM**

**@RHKIDSGRAPHIC**

Vikram Madan grew up in India, where he really wanted to be a cartoonist but ended up an engineer. After many years in the tech industry, he finally came to his senses and followed his heart back to humor. He lives near Seattle, where—in addition to making whimsical and humorous visual art—he writes and illustrates books of funny poems, including the *Kirkus Reviews* Best Book *A Hatful of Dragons* and the Moonbeam Award Winners *The Bubble Collector* and *Lord of the Bubbles*. Visit him at VikramMadan.com.

Nicola Slater lives with her family in the wild and windy north of England. She has illustrated many middle-grade novels and picture books, including *Where Is My Pink Sweater?* (which she also wrote), *Leaping Lemmings!*, *A Skunk in My Bunk!*, and Margaret Wise Brown's *Manners,* a Little Golden Book. In her spare time she likes looking at animals, camping in the rain, and tickling her children. You can follow her on Twitter at @nicolaslater.